Love, in Spanish
A novel
By Karina Halle

\m/ Metal Blonde Books \m/

First edition published by
Metal Blonde Books November 2014

Cover design by Najla Qamber
Edited by Kara Malinczak
Photographer: Scott Hoover

ISBN-13: 978-1502945266

Metal Blonde Books
P.O. Box 845
Point Roberts, WA
98281 USA

Manufactured in the USA
For more information visit:
http://authorkarinahalle.com/

For all those who heard it was impossible and went for it anyway. Love is always worth it.

Prologue

I am in love with a villain.

At least, she calls herself a villain. I'm not sure if the meaning is lost in translation—Vera does speak with a lot of English slang—or if she is being literal. But I do not see her as a villain. I see her as a girl, as a woman, as a friend, and as a lover. I see her as my star, one she thinks has burned too much for the both of us.

She is not wrong. We both have burned, and in some ways, gladly. There have been many risks that were worth taking and many times that we have fallen, but we always fall together. Our journey has never been easy. The only thing easy in all of this is my love for her. It is pure, it is simple, and it is true.

One would think that after all we have been through together, the tears and the torment, the witch hunts and the slander, at some point the path would become clear, smooth, and even.

But the road only twists and turns. It is forever uphill, forever testing us.

Through it all we have each other, two exiled souls. We pay for our sins with each kiss, we feel our mistakes with each touch.

And despite all that, I fear the day when it all becomes easy.

I fear that's the day when she'll be taken away.

My lover, my friend, my star.

She can only shine for so long.

Until she is gone for good.

Chapter One

My dearest Estrella,

    I am writing this letter in hopes you will one day read it. I am not sure if I have the strength to place it in your hand, or if you'll read this from home in Canada. That is your home, is it not? Not here, with me in Madrid. I don't deserve that. I would ask for you to pardon my English but I believe you have pardoned enough of me so far.

    All I can say is that I'm sorry. Lo siento, lo siento, lo siento. And it is not enough. I know it is not enough. To tell you how much my heart is bleeding with you gone is not enough. To tell you that you are my stars and my moon and my universe...it is not enough. I don't know if anything will be enough to take back the pain I have caused you. I don't know if anything will be enough to make things right.

I am wounded, my dear angel, and I fear you are wounded too.

I will not make excuses. But I will explain where I went wrong and why it happened. It doesn't change anything, but if you can understand the shoes I am in, maybe you will know...

I never wanted to hurt you.

I know you saw me and Isabel on the street. When I looked up, I saw you running away. You stand out on the streets of Madrid like a sore thumb, but that does not sound very flattering, does it? Funny little phrase. You stand out—always—to me. I feel as if we are connected in ways I cannot even begin to understand, and when you are near, I know. My heart races. It is a peculiar thing, this heart, is it not?

I know that after the night before, seeing me kiss her must have hurt like an arrow in your chest. But nothing is the way that you see it. But before I begin, I must go back. I must start from where I think the threads began to unravel.

When we first parted ways in Las Palabras, I knew I would see you again. I knew I would do whatever I had to in order to bring you back into my life. When I said I couldn't see the stars from the city, I was not kidding. The skies here are dark and grey, and so was my heart, so was my life.

Chloe Ann was the only bright spot in my day, and soon I knew I had to make a decision. Do I stay with Isabel for my daughter's sake? Or do I risk it for you?

As you know, I risked it. I figured, vainly perhaps, that if I stayed unhappy with Isabel, Chloe Ann would be able to tell and she would be unhappy too. Children are smarter than we give them credit for, are they not? And so I thought I had to end it. I was not happy. I knew Isabel was not happy. There was more to my black and white world than the path I was supposed to stick to.

You brought me colors and stars and cosmos and wonders. I wanted you so badly, craved you so much, that I knew I would suffer whatever bad things would come my way. There would be repercussions for my actions—I knew this, and I knew no one but you would understand.

Life is full of hard choices.

I chose you.

Isabel could hardly believe it. I can't blame her. In some ways, I couldn't believe it either. That I was doing this, taking this step, and risking it all on you. You, Vera, were the unknown. You still are. But I had faith in what we had, that our connection was more than lust and romance...it was deeper and brighter than that.

No one believed me. Why should they? They see it happen all the time, the man approaching middle-age, trading in his wife for a younger one. They said I was thinking with my cock, that I was caught up in the sex and the shiny new thing that you were. Of course, I was enamored with you, of course the sex was better than I could have ever imagined. But they didn't understand the truth behind all of it. They didn't believe I was in love with you.

I don't even think you believed it. But of course I am, more now than ever. And love makes you do silly things.

In what you would call hindsight, I see now that it was reckless and impulsive of me to ask you to move to Spain. I should have waited until the divorce was final. I should have waited until you were out of school.

I was foolish and very selfish and very scared. I could only see you, only think of you. I just wanted you here so badly, and I was afraid that if I waited, you would leave me. You would find someone better, someone your own age with less baggage. Sometimes it surprises me that you could even want me at all.

But you did. You agreed to come here, and even though I knew deep down it would be better for everyone if we waited until the dust settled, I risked it. I would have walked over burning coals for you, just to have you in my arms. I would have put the whole world in jeopardy just to be inside you again.

I should have been the adult here. I should have known better. But my heart got the best of me. I brought you here, right into the flames. I thought I could shelter you from the heat, that I could protect you, that I could ride out the inferno with you safely under my arm.

But I was wrong. And because of my recklessness, you had to suffer. I had to suffer. My daughter had to suffer. Everyone is suffering.

And you are gone.

The other night when Isabel showed up, that was the hardest night of my life, harder than the night we made love at Las Palabras, knowing we had to say goodbye the next day.

I never wanted it to happen that way. I never wanted Isabel to see you, nor you to see her. I knew you were already wrapped in guilt, and I knew Isabel would only hurt. She is a beautiful woman and she is still young. But seeing you—so fresh and shining so brightly, it would have only destroyed her, made her feel old, weak, useless. Those feelings would turn to anger, and her anger is a sharp and dangerous object.

But you came to the lobby—I cannot fault your curiosity—and the two of you met. Isabel was destroyed, and her drunken anger took over. You could only watch.

I could only watch.

I wanted to defend you. In my heart I did. But to your eyes I didn't. I couldn't.

I told you that one day I'd have to choose between you and Chloe Ann. I suppose at that moment, I had to make that choice. I had to play right by Isabel. I couldn't choose you, because if I did, I would lose all contact with Chloe Ann. I was at Isabel's mercy, and she had me by the balls.

It is complicated. It is so complicated. All these threads and knots wrapped around all of our necks, tying us to one another. If one moves, the other feels it, loses air. I defended Isabel, and the rope tightened around your throat. If I defended you, the rope would be severed between me and my daughter.

I cannot expect you to understand. You are not a parent. You don't have to make the horrible choices—or maybe you do. Maybe you just made a horrible choice of your own by leaving me. All I can say is there is no winning. How do you choose between your own flesh and blood and the love of your life? You can't really…I could only choose because Chloe Ann is young and needs me. She wouldn't understand the choice. But you, Vera, you might understand. You might see where I am coming from. You might be able to forgive me.

Please forgive me.

That night I went back home. I don't feel I have to assure you that nothing happened between Isabel and I—but nothing did happen. I talked to Chloe Ann. I tried to make as much peace with Isabel as I could in her drunken state. I at least got her to calm down. I slept on the couch.

The next morning, I woke up early and made breakfast. The three of us sat together, as a family, for the last time. Isabel was terribly hung over but she had softened. Perhaps she finally saw how over it was and how there would be no us, no going back. What was done was done.

So we put on sad smiles and ate, and Chloe Ann was delighted to have us all back together. Our smiles got sadder.

Then Isabel drove me home.

You see, love is a strange thing. It can disappear completely. It can leave you, so far gone it is just a mark on the horizon, and you wonder how you ever felt love to begin with. But even with it gone, fragments still remain. There are imprints. You can destroy a house and ruin it to the ground but you'll see indents in the earth, the way the ground is different where the house once was.

We talked, Isabel and I, for a long time. She was still angry, bitter, as I expect she'll be for a long time. I would be too, if I were in her shoes. Perhaps this is what makes everything so much harder, that I know how others see me, that what I've done is reprehensible to them. But she had relented to what was, to the new reality. And in our words about the past and the present and the future, I could see the remains of what once was, see the ghost of our marriage, that time when we had a bit of hope for each other.

I am not in love with Isabel. I am in love with you. I do not even love Isabel. I love you. But for that moment, I cared about her more than I had in a long time. I worried for her. I wanted to make things right, even though it seemed impossible. Perhaps it was because I knew this was really the end, and it was time for us both to move on for good.

I kissed her goodbye without a second thought. It is in my nature to be physical. It is in my nature to be tender. There was no meaning in it except for sinking into old habits and the bittersweet notion of saying goodbye. You see, though I no longer love Isabel, the ghost of the marriage still remained. I said goodbye to that ghost.

Of course, I know how that all looked to you, and I cannot blame you for running, blame you for leaving. Things had gotten hard, and I was shouldering so much, hoping you could shoulder it too. I should have never put you in this position and dragged you all the way here when things were so unbalanced, but fools are those who fall in love, and I was a fool. I still am. And for any grief and pain I have caused you, my dearest Estrella, I am deeply sorry.

All I can say is, if I ever get a chance again, I will not mess it up. I will be good to you. I will be better than good. And I will fight. Even if you pull away, I will pull you back. I just hope you have enough room in your heart for a tired old fool like me who still makes mistakes when he should know better.

I love you.

Come back to me, my Estrella.

Mateo.

I stare at the letter in my hands as I do every night when I wake up and can't fall back asleep. I can barely see from the light filtering in through the curtains, but I know every word, every sentence, by heart. This is to remind me what I'm fighting for, to remind me how hard it was when Vera left me nearly a year ago.

I never gave her the letter. I've explained, in person, the feelings I expressed in it. I brushed away her doubts when they came crawling—she has so many of them sometimes. But I never gave it to her. There was no need. I wrote the letter and sat in my apartment, my head in my hands, my heart breaking, and I realized it wasn't enough.

Vera deserved more than just a letter. She deserved everything I had. With some difficulty I was able to speak with Vera's brother and mother in Vancouver and offer to buy her flight home. I told her mother— prickly thing that she is—that Vera needed to be with family, those that love her.

I love her. She is my family.

It was a gamble. I didn't know if she'd even be on the plane, let alone willing to forgive me. So I took the time to make sure everything was right. I spoke to Isabel, several times, and did my best to try and get her to see my point of view. I didn't want to lose joint custody of Chloe Ann; I didn't want her to grow up without a father.

Isabel almost relented. It took padding the settlement with extra cash to finally get her to agree. Of course, it was worth it. To have my daughter, I would have paid anything.

To have Vera back, I would have done everything.

Once I was at the airport, I waited in the background as the plane boarded. I was sure I looked suspicious, but I didn't want to give Vera a reason to back out. I felt her before I saw her, her aura pulling me in like gravity. She looked absolutely beautiful, so much so that I could barely stand on my own two feet and watch as she walked past. Radiant pain spread through my chest, and I was certain I was having a heart attack. But it was just the impact of seeing her and the pain that I might still lose her in the end.

I'm normally a confident man—my career has instilled that in me. But at that moment, I felt drained of it. I headed to the washroom to splash water on my face. I stared at myself in the mirror and didn't see a confident man in a sharp suit. I saw a little boy whose heart lay in someone else's hands.

I walked on the plane last minute and readied myself as I made my way down the aisle. I ignored the annoyed stares of the people who had to wait for me, and held my breath until I saw her.

Vera's body was angled toward the window, her hair covering her face. She looked both small and wild, and I itched to touch those shiny curls that ran down her back, the color of orange cream. The woman on the aisle was staring at me with blatant disappointment—she thought she wouldn't have anyone sitting next to her the whole trip. Little did she know, all my attention would be on the other seat during the flight.

My patience was tested. I sat there, still as stone, my eyes solely on Vera, during taxi, take-off, when we reached cruising altitude. From the way her back rose and the occasional quiet whimper that escaped, I knew she was crying. It took everything I had not to break down myself. I wanted to kiss those tears away.

But I would wait for her to discover me.

Finally, she did. She adjusted herself in her seat and elbowed me. I'd never smiled so wide.

"Sorry," she mumbled in her wonderful smoky voice, still not turning around.

I licked my lips and breathed in deeply before I said, "I am sorry too."

Her body stiffened. She slowly turned her head, and my smile grew soft at the sight of her reddened eyes and the tracks of tears beneath them. She looked impossibly stunned, like she'd seen a ghost. Only I was no apparition; I was real.

Instead of giving her the letter, I opened up and laid it all out there for her to see, no stone unturned. The thing I was most afraid of was having my heart, my love rejected, for her to turn her back. It was her right to do so, and yet I wished for nothing more than another chance.

But Vera, such a generous, willing soul, didn't reject me. She gave me love in return, love that she said had never left her.

We landed in Vancouver to see her mother and brother, Josh, at the airport. Naturally they were surprised to see me, and I was surprised to see them—at least her mother. She had sounded so harsh and cold over the phone, yet there she was, waiting for her daughter to return, shocked that the adulterer was by her side. If looks could kill, I would have turned to ash right there on the airport floor.

It wasn't an easy couple of days. I was glad I had packed that letter in my carry-on, because it reminded me to hold on. Her mother and sister and future brother-in-law from England all seemed to despise me, especially when they realized that we were heading right back to Madrid. At one point, the English asshole pulled me aside and asked me why I couldn't go back to my wife and leave a young girl like Vera alone.

I nearly punched him in the face, but I knew that wouldn't help our case. Vera and I were used to being sneered at by this point, and though she said she didn't care what her family thought, I could still see it in the way she carried herself that she did. Even though it had waned since I met her, the need for her family's approval was still there.

Thank god for Josh, who was the only smart, kind, and decent one in her family. With his black edgy hair and tattoos, he was definitely one of those people you wanted to judge before you knew them, but he was Vera's biggest supporter and the saving grace for our brief stay.

That wasn't the last time we'd see them, though. Just after Christmas we went back, but this time we had reinforcements—our friends Claudia and Ricardo. We went primarily so that Vera could send in her work permit application that Las Palabras had arranged, but the ski trip to Whistler with everyone, including Josh, didn't hurt. A week blasting down the slopes and relaxing with friends and family seemed to be just the thing we needed.

When we left it was still a bit up in the air whether Vera would return to Vancouver for her sister's wedding in July or not. I told her I would go with her if she did, if she wanted me to, and I'd support her if she didn't. In the end, she opted to stay in Spain, and I think she pissed off her family once again. It was also up in the air whether Vera would actually get a work permit through Las Palabras. But there were other routes she could take in order to stay and work in the country, and in the end the Spanish government granted her six months at Las Palabras and to reapply again when the time was up. Either way, she wouldn't have to leave Spain if she didn't want to.

And yet, as she lies beside me, sleeping silently in the night's hazy wash of indigo, I have this unsettled feeling deep in my chest. It's what has kept me up all month, more so than the stifling August heat. It's this feeling that everything is about to change for us.

It's partly my fault, although the change is for what I hope is the better. Over the last six months, we've settled into a steady and comfortable routine. Vera works at Las Palabras from 9 a.m. till 2 p.m. most days of the week, and though it's just an office job, she seems to enjoy it. She takes Spanish classes on Tuesday nights. She has her friends, Claudia and Ricardo, plus a few others from the program, and her new job. Chloe Ann lives with Isabel but I get her Wednesdays and either Saturday or Sunday. Isabel is cold but courteous to me, and she's only had to interact with Vera once or twice. It's awkward for everyone—it always is—but it works for now.

But for me, things have become a little too stagnant. Falling in love with Vera and escaping an unhappy marriage has opened my mind, my soul, up to myriad of possibilities. The restaurant business wasn't for me anymore, and it isn't where my passion lies, so I sold it to my partner. What I really want is to feel that excitement again, the one I had when I was younger and believed I could do anything. I want something else in my life to fulfill me the way the love of Vera and Chloe Ann does.

I really didn't think it was possible, but after the paparazzi got a whiff of my divorce and Vera and I started showing up unceremoniously in the tabloids, my face got back out there. From one ugly thing a promising start was born.

A few months ago I was contacted by my old football team—Atlético Madrid—and asked if I had any interest in the team anymore. The fact that I was turning thirty-nine and still had my knee injury didn't seem to matter. They didn't want me to play for them—they knew that my time in the sun had set—but they wanted to know if I could somehow involve myself with the organization. Perhaps they thought my newfound attention would help bolster theirs, I don't know, but suddenly I was worth something to them.

At first it was a few meetings, a couple of chats here and there. With the coach, then the general manager, then the owner. Maybe I wanted to donate some money, host an event, become a mentor. They were full of ideas at first. Then it led to talks about assistant coaching, which after a while petered off.

I tried not to get my hopes up, but like most things in life, the hope sneaks in. I felt acute disappointment when I hadn't heard from them and poor Vera had to put up with my moping around the apartment for days on end.

That was until Friday afternoon, when I got a phone call from the manager. They wanted me to meet them for lunch at Fioris Café on Monday, which it technically is right now, to discuss an urgent matter.

It's no wonder that I can't sleep. I only pray it's just my nerves that are having their way with me, that there is no real reason for the sense of foreboding that I have.

Vera turns over in our bed, her hair spilling around her face, her breasts nearly coming free of the delicate straps of her top. Her skin is white silk scattered with colorful art. I'd never really found tattoos sexy until I met her and saw the way they shaped her, how they represented a million stories, emotions, expressions.

Her eyes slowly flutter open and she stares at me with this hazy, sleepy look. "What are you doing?" she asks softly.

I slip the letter back in the drawer. I know she's seen me reading it before. She's never asked what it is, but I can tell she knows it means something to me and I respect that. I would gladly show her the letter, but the reason why I'm reading it may be unnerving for her. She's been a bit on edge lately, like someone is ready to pull the rug out from under her, and I don't want to give her anything else to worry about.

My fears are just that—*my* fears. She shouldn't have to shoulder them.

"I couldn't sleep," I tell her with a small smile. I get off the chair and stretch, my arms high above my head. Her eyes widen appreciatively at the sight of me. I've started sleeping in the nude.

She pulls her eyes away long enough to ask, "Are you nervous about tomorrow?"

I nod, letting out a small sigh, and come over to the bed, climbing back under the covers, which is comprised of just a sheet now in these hot August nights. I lay my head on the pillow and stare into her eyes, pushing back strands of silk hair behind her ears.

She gives me a reassuring smile. "Don't worry about it. I'm sure whatever they want to talk to you about is a good thing."

"I hope so," I admit.

"I *know* so."

I grin at her. "You seem to know so much in the middle of the night."

She cocks a brow. "Didn't you know? I'm at my best at this time. Want me to show you?"

I can never say no to that. Her lids become heavy, mouth full, wet and parted in anticipation. That suggestive look is all I need to become hard.

She leans over and kisses me softly. My tongue explores her mouth in a luxurious fashion, slowly building a hot need between us. While my hand slips to the back of her neck, pulling her toward me, her fingers trail from the rough stubble on my chin down my chest and the firm ridges of my stomach, and wrap around my stiff cock.

I groan, closing my eyes to her grip as she makes a fist and lightly skims the length of me up and down.

"If you keep doing that," I manage to say against her mouth, "the show will be over pretty quickly."

She chuckles and pulls away, her lips skirting my chin, neck, chest. "As long as I give you a good show, I don't mind."

Normally when one of us wakes up in the middle of the night feeling amorous, a sleepy, hazy form of sex takes place. One of the best kinds of sex. But if she's willing and wanting to give me a blow job, I have no inclination to stop her. A true gentleman never stops a woman from doing what she desires.

Her lips slide down from my stomach to the tip of my shaft, and she takes me whole and deep into her mouth. I don't know where Vera learned her skills—and I never want to know—but I'm eternally grateful for them. With her mouth, tongue, and hand working in unison, I succumb to the sensation, the warmth flooding through my limbs. My fingers curl into her hair, gripping tight.

When her other hand goes to my balls, cupping them with just enough pressure to drive me wild, I can't help but yank at her hair. "Fuck," I whimper. "Oh fuck, Vera. Fuck yes. More."

She picks up the pace, and I begin thrusting my hips up, my cock going as deep into her throat as possible, her lips enveloping me like a velvet glove. I come hard and she doesn't pull away, doesn't stop until there's nothing left in me.

I'm left panting on the bed, the waves bringing me deeper into the mattress, my hands letting go of her hair. I hear her swallow and wipe her lips, like the wonderfully bad girl that she is, and I open my eyes to see her smiling at me in the dim light. She looks awfully proud of herself, as she should.

"Your turn," I tell her, trying to get up, but she pushes her hand into my chest so I'm lying back down.

"You can deal with me tomorrow," she says, taking a sip of water. "I'm exhausted. Your cock takes a lot of work there, big boy."

I can't help but grin at her flattering choice of words. "You spoil me."

She smiles like she knows it's true then kisses me quickly on the lips before rolling over on her side so her back is to me. I scoop my arms around her waist and pull her into me, not wanting to fall asleep without her in my arms.

A few moments pass and our breathing lengthens. Outside, a car putters down the street. Everything else is quiet.

"I love you," I whisper into her ear.

My voice seems to echo in the room. She's already asleep.

Chapter Two

"So Mateo," Pedro del Torro says as he spoons sugar into his black coffee and gives it a methodical stir. "Do you have any idea of why we might have asked you here today?"

I am sitting across from him and the diminutive Antonio Ramos in one of Madrid's more prestigious cafés. Nothing but the best for these two, although Antonio has only been the general manager for about three years. As Atletico's owner, Pedro flaunts his power and money like it's no one's business, more so when the team is doing well, like they have been.

I give them a shrug and a half-smile. "Because you find me charming?"

Pedro breaks into an easy laugh, one that I can't tell is for show or not. He takes a sip of his coffee and nods appreciatively at it. "The coffee here never lets me down. That's why I keep coming back for more."

I stare at him, knowing I have to humor his indulgences before he gets down to business.

"You, Mateo," he goes on, "seem to be the same. Reliable. The kind of *person* that doesn't let anyone down."

I keep my expression neutral. God knows that I've let enough people down in my lifetime.

He leans forward and folds his leathered hands in front of him. "Diego is leaving the team in January."

I raise my brows in surprise. Diego Martinez is the coach, and a great one at that. He's helped bring the team back from the brink all those years ago.

"Why?" I ask, trying to ignore the feeling inside me, like my chest is taking flight. I can't get ahead of myself here, can't dare dream of where this could be leading.

Pedro exchanges a tired glance with Antonio before turning his sharp eyes back to me. "He's going to coach for the Argentina team instead. We've known about it for a while, we just weren't sure what to do about it."

I clear my throat and fight the urge to straighten the cuffs on my rolled up sleeves. "And Warren?" Warren is the assistant coach, a Brit who used to play for Arsenal way back in the day. For a while there, with all these meetings, I had thought that perhaps I was being groomed to take his position. Now it has the possibility to be so much more than that.

"We had hopes that Warren would be able to step up. But the truth is, we'd all want a Spaniard in charge of the boys and one from the *family*." Pedro pauses to take another sip of coffee and wipes delicately at his mustache before saying, "We want you, Mateo."

I blink at him. "Me?"

"Yes," he says with a quick smile. "Naturally you realized we wanted to do business with you."

I sit back in my chair, faintly aware that my heart is pounding loudly in my ears. "Well, yes, but there is business and there is being a coach of an international football team. I don't mean to sound ungrateful, but what makes you think this is something I can do? I haven't been in the game for a long time."

Pedro and Antonio exchange another look, and this time Antonio speaks, slow and measured. "We think you'll do just fine. We have until January, of course, and will put you in with Warren and Diego immediately. You'll get a feel for it, what it's like to be back. Believe me, Mateo, I used to watch you play religiously, and for someone like you, this is a natural progression."

"Besides," Pedro adds, "it's always good to mix things up. With Diego leaving, we want to ensure that the players and the audience are riveted as always. Having a player like you back in the saddle, so to speak, would attract a lot of attention to the team. Especially since you've been in the public eye again this past year."

I swallow and give him an uneasy smile. He doesn't seem too pleased about that, how the paparazzi went a little crazy over my divorce, and the scandal of dating a younger, foreign woman. I wait for Pedro to bring up Vera, but he doesn't.

"You don't have to give us your answer now," he says smoothly, his face going from stern contempt to one of a crafty politician. "We have plenty of time. How about you let us know by the end of the week and we'll take the next steps from there? This will no doubt change your life, Mateo, but only for the better."

Lunch is served soon after and their talks turn to the sport, to films, to the weather. I smile and nod but I am trapped inside my head. One part of me feels ready to burst from happiness, from the prospect of fulfillment, while another part is digging its nails in, afraid to let go, afraid of more change.

We leave the restaurant together, and I tell them I'll give them a call on Friday. They wave me off as if they know my answer already. Perhaps I know it too. Still, I share my life with Vera and would not act without discussing it with her, even if I was one hundred percent certain.

We get two steps down the cracked concrete stairs before a flashbulb goes off in my face. A slim photographer with a long mullet is crouching down, taking our picture. I've seen him before, snapping shots of me and Vera on our nights out but that was months and months ago.

"Why is Mateo Casalles meeting with Atlético?" the photographer asks but Pedro just smiles and raises his hand in a slight wave before turning to the left. I go right, and the photographer follows me, an easy target.

"Are you joining Atlético again, Mateo?" he persists, and I turn slightly to give him a look.

"Don't you have anything better to do?" I say, and keep walking. He doesn't bother following me beyond the corner.

By the time I'm back at the apartment, the sun is overbearing, and the streets, even in our neighborhood, the elegant Salamanca *barrio*, smell like garbage and dust. The building offers a cool respite, and when I open the door to our flat, Vera is standing in the gleaming kitchen, stirring a pitcher of lemonade.

"Aren't you a sight for sore eyes?" I ask as I put my keys on the table, remembering the particular English phrase.

She turns to me and gives me a big smile. She looks like a housewife from the 1950s with the eyes of a femme fatale. She's squeezed herself into a fitted strapless yellow dress that shows off her full breasts and wide hips, and has a silk patterned scarf pulling her voracious hair off her forehead. But her tattoos and black high-top sneakers remind me that she's not like any other housewife I know.

"Very good," she says, always pleased when I remember the idiosyncrasies of her language. She raises the pitcher. "Don't worry, there's vodka in it."

I grin at her and wrap my arms around her waist, pulling her up against me. "Of course there is."

She yelps as a bit of the lemonade splashes over the side and onto the floor but I don't let go. She manages to put the pitcher down before I bury my face in her neck, nipping and kissing at her delicate skin. She tastes like sunshine and citrus.

"So," she says breathlessly, and I can feel her pulse quickening beneath my lips. I run my hand over the slope of her ass and give it a hard squeeze as I press myself against her. "Do I have to ask how it went?"

"I will tell you all about it," I murmur, "later. But you're wearing that dress and making me drunken lemonade on this hot day, and I'm afraid I'll have to deal with you first."

I bring my lips to the space behind her ear where her newest tattoo is. It says, in Spanish, *Love, in Spanish is you*, something I said to Vera back in La Alberca when I was first falling for her. It remains true to this day. I run the tip of my tongue over the words, and she shudders beneath me. She can never resist that, though she never seems to resist anything.

I love that about her.

I grab hold of the zipper at the back of her dress and slowly start pulling it down until her breasts are free.

I cup them, my mouth grazing her nipples that pucker beneath me. I take my time, wanting to enjoy every minute with them in this bright light, this cool kitchen, this hot city.

She moans as I run my tongue around in deliberate circles, and she starts to run her fingers through my hair, tugging on it gently. It ignites nerves that shoot directly to my cock but I'm already hard as steel and straining against my pants.

With one smooth motion I pick her up and place her over my shoulder, caveman-style. She lets out a little laugh, playfully kicking her toes against my stomach and pounding her fists against my back. "Put me down, you bad man," she says in mock distress.

I give her an exaggerated grunt and then drop her on the couch. She doesn't have time to adjust herself; I'm on her in a second, pulling the dress over her head and discarding it on the coffee table. I stare down at her body lying against the cushions, pale and soft and all for me, and grab hold of her calves, yanking her toward me until her ass and hips are propped up against the armrest, her legs dangling over the sides.

"Get naked," she commands me, but I only give her a half-smile. I'll get naked, after I'm done with the first course. She always comes first. That is the rule, even though she broke it last night with those irresistible lips of hers.

I get down on my knees and pull her hips even closer toward me, her pussy is bare, wet and waiting. It's beautiful. I trail my lips and tongue from the inside of her knee—something that solicits a breathy groan from her—and up the silky path of her inner thighs. She arches her back, pushing herself into my mouth greedily.

She tastes good—like her, like the ocean and youth—and I take my time running my tongue around her clit, up and down the curves before plunging it inside her.

"Mateo," she says between groans. "Oh god, don't stop."

I grin and pull away from her, doing just the opposite. "Speak to me in Spanish, my Estrella, and I'll continue."

I watch her close her eyes and arch her neck. "Fuck me with your mouth, harder, deeper," she says in broken Spanish. It's the sexiest thing I have ever heard. Her Spanish lessons are really paying off.

Naturally, I comply, my fingers joining in so that she's coming hard within seconds. She cries out, as if the orgasm has taken her by surprise, and I can feel her quivers racing beneath my lips and around my fingers.

I straighten up and stare down at her spent body as I unbutton my shirt. "*Now*, I'll get naked."

I swiftly remove it and my pants until it's just me and my erection in front of her. She lifts her head, eying my body appreciatively, the hunger reappearing and ready for more. She's insatiable.

"Turn around," I tell her, and she immediately responds by getting on her hands and knees on the couch, her ripe, round ass facing me. She moves forward to make room, and I get right behind her, one leg on the floor, bracing my weight, the other on the couch. I wrap one hand around her waist and relish the sight of it, my long, bronzed fingers standing out against the creamy white of her skin.

I knead at her waist, her ass, the soft slope of her thighs, taking my time, building the anticipation for both of us. When she starts to shift, her patience wearing thin, I bring my fingers up through her slickness, lightly pressing on her clit for a moment then taking my hand away. She's wanting it, her back arched, ass pressed toward me, begging for it, but it's now my game we are playing. In my game, it is not all about the goal. A silly analogy for a football player, perhaps, but when it comes to sex it is the truth.

I take her wetness and use it to lubricate my hand as I stroke myself. I bring my fist up and down my cock and close my eyes, carefully stoking the fire inside me. I can hear her whimper, wanting to see, to be involved. It's all part of the journey.

Finally, when I'm getting too close to orgasm for my own good, I start teasing the crack of her ass with the tip, and the slight pressure makes her moan.

"God, Mateo, please."

I smile to myself. "That sounds like English."

"Por favor," she begs, her accent perfect.

I press it against her, feeling her spread for me, but I don't push in yet. Teasing is just too much fun.

"Por favor, Mateo," she cries out in frustration. "Dios mio."

She calls me her God.

"Si, Estrella," I tell her, and with one swift motion, I push inside of her. She feels like heat and honey, and as I drive myself in deep, I feel my breath and heartbeat catch in the back of my throat. The headiness swarms around me, begging for more, as I thrust harder, faster. My balls smack her ass—in my delirium it sounds like angels—and the need to come inside her, to plant my seed deep, takes over.

My grip on her hips tightens, and I hold on as I pound her again and again. She cries out, swept away by the same frenzy. The couch rattles loudly against the wall, and when my thrusts become more powerful, it starts to move along the floor, inch by inch. I have never wanted to fuck her so hard, so intensely, than I do in this moment, as if biological urges and frivolous desire were melded into one driving life force.

I feel as if I am nailing her to some place—perhaps this world, this moment, and I want nothing more than to be so deep that I leave some permanent reminder of myself. She is mine, all mine; she is mine now and forever, this beautiful, soft, wet woman of my dreams and my heart, and I am going to fuck her until she's screaming my name.

It doesn't take long. She lets out this low, guttural moan that builds to a crescendo, and as she throbs around me, squeezing my cock with her lengthy shudders, I let go. I come hard, and for a long time my face is contorted, my nonsensical cries hissing out of my mouth in short bursts of painful euphoria.

When I am finally milked dry, I pull out and collapse on the couch beside her, pulling her up against my chest. We are both breathing hard but I still kiss the top of her neck and hold her close to me so our sweat mingles and mixes, and our limbs wrap around each other. I am outside of her but we are still one.

The clock on the wall ticks away and we lie here for twenty minutes, not saying anything, just breathing, just being. I don't know why she sometimes turns me into such a Neanderthal, but when it ends in such away, I don't see either of us complaining about it.

Eventually she lifts her head and looks up at me with hazel eyes that are both exhausted and bright. "So," she says, nestling her hands into my chest, "now that we've got the fucking-your-brains-out out of the way, will you tell me about your day? Or are you holding that information hostage for more sexual encounters? Because as eager as I am for anything that involves your cock, my cooch is a bit sore from that pounding."

"Cooch?" I ask, puzzled but smiling at the sound of the word on my lips.

She shrugs. "Coño."

I shake my head slightly. "I am not sure I like this cooch. It sounds like a cartoon character, a name far too silly for something as serious as your pussy."

She grins at me and her face lights up like a sparkler. "I have a serious pussy?"

"Well, let's just say I take your pussy very seriously," I say. I run my thumb over her lips and then say, "Today went very well. Pedro, the owner, and Antonio, they want me to take over Diego's position in January. They want me to be the coach."

Her eyes widen into shining pools. "Are you serious?"

"As serious as your pussy."

"Mateo," she exclaims, pushing herself up. "They want you to be coach? What about that other guy, the English dude?"

"Warren? They aren't too sure about him. They want a Spaniard and a former teammate to have the job. Diego is leaving to coach Argentina in the new year so I am to be his replacement. I will have all this time to learn and see if I can do the job."

"Of course you can do the job," Vera says, though the only time she's seen me play was in Las Palabras, where I failed miserably thanks to my knee, and a few old Atlético games that someone uploaded onto YouTube. "You can do anything."

I cock my head, considering that. "I don't know," I say unsurely. "I am a bit rusty. I have never coached. I don't know how to lead."

She is staring at me like I could never let her down. I'm not sure if I like it. "Oh, Mateo. You have no idea, do you?"

"What?"

"You don't know how to lead," she repeats, mocking it. "In Las Palabras, you were always the leader. Everyone gravitated toward you because they recognized that. Do you not remember your own presentation about creating your own destiny? That's what you do, Mateo. You create. You lead. Everyone else follows."

"I follow you," I tell her, kissing the tip of her nose.

"You follow my coño," she says.

I place my hands on either side of her face and hold her as I stare deep into her eyes. "I follow every part of you, everywhere. You go before me, Vera. You always will."

As she sometimes does when I'm being especially honest, she looks away shyly. It's cute, like she can't believe that I could feel the way that I do about her. But sometimes, most times, I just want her to believe it, to own it.

"Anyway," she says, quickly skirting over what I said, "you do have what it takes, Mateo. I think this could be the best thing that could happen to you. You'll be a part of what you love again, in it as much as you can be. But it's not about what I think."

"It is about what you think."

"It's about what *you* think," she says. "So what did you tell them?"

I lay my head back against the couch cushions and stare at the ceiling. "They are giving me until Friday to think about it."

"Good," she says. "By then you'll know what you want, if not sooner."

But the thing is, all I really want is her.

Somehow, the night seems to be hotter than the day. The air is thick and sweltering, like simmering soup, as Vera and I walk hand in hand to my parents' front door. They

39

have no air-conditioning inside and I'm already chastising myself for wearing a suit, but even pushing forty, it's hard not to dress up for your parents. My mother had instilled it in me at a young age, to always look nice for her, if not for my father, and it's something I do now for Carmen, my stepmother.

We stand on the front steps and I squeeze Vera's hand appreciatively. We have dinner at their house usually once a month, on whatever day my sister Lucia can fit into her social calendar. Vera gets along very well with my parents, especially now that she's picked up a bit of Spanish and can converse more with my non-English speaking father. Originally she was going to try teaching him English but my father has the patience of a cat, and that never amounted to anything.

Carmen opens the door with a bright smile on her face, the smell of anchovies and basil wafting in from behind her. She's quite a bit younger than my father, but no matter her age, she seems to give off this air of vitality. I think she keeps my father young. She definitely keeps the old grump on his toes.

"Mateo," she cries out, and pulls me into a hard embrace. She smells like sage and earth, and her large earrings rattle as she pulls away, holding me at arm's length while she looks me over, as if I am just a boy and not a man. I don't mind.

She sweeps her eyes to Vera and takes her in like a cool glass of water. It helps that Vera is dressed in a metallic silver shift dress, the kind you'd see in a futuristic version of the 1960s.

"Vera," she says, "you look beautiful. Your dress, you're really becoming quite stylish."

Vera waves away the compliment as pink stains the apples of her cheeks. "Blame it on Spain," she says with a smile. It's true though, shopping in the winding alleyways of Madrid with her friend Claudia has become one of her favorite activities, and every day her own sense of style and well-being seems to blossom.

I am aware that I am beaming at Vera proudly when Carmen pinches my cheek quickly and says in Spanish, "You're still as smitten as the first time. That makes me happy, Mateo."

Vera shoots me an inquisitive glance but I only press my hand into her lower back and usher her inside the house.

There is a fan in every room, their constant whirring competing with the sultry sounds of Ella Fitzgerald on the record player. My father is sitting in the living room with a glass of wine beside an open bottle, leaning back in his chair, eyes closed.

"Ignore him," Carmen says, gesturing for us to sit down while she places two extra glasses beside the bottle. "He's pretending to be asleep. He's mad at me because I wouldn't let him put extra anchovies into the sauce."

Sure enough, the moment she turns and heads back into the kitchen, my father opens one eye in a rather comedic gesture.

"Don't worry, she's gone," Vera says in Spanish as I pour ourselves some wine.

My father smirks at her appreciatively and my chest feels warm. I never have any doubts when it comes to our relationship, but I know most people do. It's tiring to have to explain why I'm with her, why she's with me, why I left my wife, how I could do such a thing.

With my parents though, they never judged me. They understood in some ways that life doesn't always hand you things in a neat package. It dollops them out here and there in messy, confusing splatters, and when you see something amazing, you better drop what you're doing and hold on with two hands. They know why I held on to Vera when I came across her and why I still haven't let go. They know that true love only comes by once, or twice, if you're really lucky.

My father was one of the especially lucky ones. He lost the love of his life—my mother—and though it took ten years, he finally found Carmen. He never gave up hope or faith that he would find someone else for him.

We are joined by Lucia, who has come straight from her new job at one of the television stations. She's lively and talkative, and drinks most of the wine, but I can't help but retreat into myself, lost in thought. Times like this, with my family, trick me into thinking the path Vera and I have chosen is an easy one. It makes me crave the warmth of a house, of a future, of my own flesh and blood.

I stare across the table at Vera as she brushes a wayward strand of hair behind her ear, her other hand tucked under her chin, her smile and kind eyes focused on Lucia as she describes her day to us with crazy hand gestures. I'm not getting any younger, but neither is Vera. I'm not with her just for the moment, she is not just a passing fancy. I want Vera by my side for the rest of my life.

It's scary to think about. Not the commitment. You would think that after one marriage and a bitter divorce, I would have sworn off the whole concept of marriage. But my situation with Isabel never tainted the institution for me. It's something I still believe in. If anything, I believe more in getting it right.

I want to get it right with Vera. It's a luxury I rarely let myself think about because there are so many unknowns, so many variables. That is what is so scary about it. What does Vera want? She's only twenty-four—she hasn't once mentioned marriage or children, or even talked about that far into the future. It's probably those reasons why she feels so temporary sometimes.

But I don't want that anymore. I want her here, with me, permanently. I don't want there to be any fears over whether she'll be around, allowed to stay in the country or otherwise. I don't want any doubts when I think about my future. I want to know she'll be there with me with that same infectious laugh that makes my heart sing, her view of the world that challenges mine and makes me face toward the light.

All that aside though, all my needs and my wants and the things I dare dream about, is the fact that I don't want to scare her off. I don't want to push anything on her that she may not be open to. Sometimes she feels like she's on a different path than mine. I want to make sure this is something she wants on her own.

She catches me watching her, and a wash of understanding slides over her eyes. I think for a moment that perhaps this is her, wanting it, but then I realize she is not a mind reader.

"Mateo got some interesting news today," she says, as if I was prompting her.

I feel the eyes of everyone on me. I raise my brows at Vera. It's true that I was going to tell them about Atlético's offer, but now it seems trivial compared to my previous thoughts. Even though it's the chance to reclaim my career, to work for passion, that only solidifies what I want.

I clear my throat. "Well, I had a meeting with the owner and general manager of Atlético today."

Everyone snaps to attention. I hadn't mentioned to them the previous times I met with them in case it turned out to be nothing, so this is a bit out of the blue. It explains how Lucia's groomed eyebrows seem halfway up her forehead.

"What about?" Carmen asks, her tone high and hesitant.

I shrug casually. "They asked me if I would become coach in January to replace Diego. He's going to Argentina. I have until Friday to decide."

They are stunned. More stunned than when I first told them I was getting a divorce. Finally my father says, "Took the fools long enough."

They are excited, happier for me than perhaps I am. They all think I could make a difference, that I'll do an excellent job, that I was meant for the position. They are not wrong in any of this.

Vera is staring at me, her red lips quirked up to the side, her eyes shining. She looks like a girl and a woman, and I want nothing more than to make her proud. I want to embrace this change but only if she's there every step of the way.

Later, after we've all eaten the custard confection that Carmen prepared for dessert and we're all sitting around with tiny glasses of my father's favorite cognac, Lucia pulls me aside. She takes me to the balcony overlooking the gardens of the backyard and the fish pond, and pulls out a cigarette.

"I thought you quit," I note, eyeing it disdainfully as she lights up. Still, I can't help but breathe in that first hint of burning tobacco paper before it disappears into the smell of tired heat and the fresh scent of the neigh-bourhood sprinklers as they whir in the night.

She rolls her eyes in a way that makes her look like a teenager. "I took it up again after Alvarez cheated on me."

Ah yes, things didn't end so well with her latest boyfriend. Not that I was surprised, since the man was a notorious player close to my age, one of those start-up business millionaires. Lucia doesn't seem to care much either, maybe that was part of the problem.

"When are you going to find a good man, some-one to settle down with?"

She laughs caustically at this and purses her lips as she eyes me expectantly. "When are *you* going to settle down?"

I narrow my eyes. "I am newly divorced, Lucia."

She tilts her head to the side but her expression doesn't change. "We all know that. And the reason you are newly divorced, Mateo…I saw the way you look at her tonight. Every time I see you, it is always the same."

I raise my hand to stop her and look out at the dark foliage of the backyard and the lights of the nearest houses. "Don't compare it to food because I've heard that one before."

"You're in love with her," she says.

I shake my head. "Your powers of deduction are impressive."

"No, Mateo," she says, and her voice is suddenly serious. "I mean, really in love. You're going to ask her to marry you, aren't you?"

Her words shock me, and I quickly eye the house to make sure no one is listening. "Can you not say that so loudly?" I ask, annoyed, more so that she's figured me out than the fact she's being so blunt about it.

"But it's true," she says between puffs. "Isn't it?"

I sigh and run my hand over my face. "Vera is not ready for that."

"How do you know, have you asked her?"

"She is too young."

"She is my age, more or less, and yet you just brought up the same question to me. How come it is something conceivable with me but not for her?"

"Because," I say slowly, "I don't wish to get my hopes up."

She leans against the railing, watching me for a beat that ticks on too long. I can feel all the conclusions she's drawing. "But your hopes are up, aren't they? Look, I love Vera. I wish I knew her better, that we'd see each other more often, but my dear brother is so selfish with her time. So I don't know her like I should. But I don't think she's going to run away from you in fear, Mateo. She's a foreigner in this country, facing an uncertain future, barely speaking the language. She's doing this all for you. Maybe you should have more faith."

I give her a look. "So is that why you brought me out here?"

She shrugs with one shoulder and blows out a cloud of smoke that hangs in the heavy air. "I was just curious. I thought, if you do, maybe I could help you pick out the ring. Be involved in some way."

Now this surprises me. Lucia and I are close, but because of our age difference, we've never been *that* close. "I see. I'm back with Atlético and now you want to be friends with your big shot brother."

She smiles at me. "So you are taking the job?"

I exhale slowly through my nose, but the doubt I felt from earlier, the doubt that holds back my words, is gone. "I don't know. But I think so. I will tell them on Friday though, just to be sure."

"Why wouldn't you take it?" she asks.

"I don't know. It could change everything, couldn't it? I would be back in the public eye again. They seemed to like harassing us an awful lot when I was no longer part of the team. How are they going to like me when I'm the coach?"

She bites her lip and gives me a sympathetic look. "You are right," she says, tapping her cigarette so the ash falls to the floor. She brushes it off the edge of the balcony with her foot to avoid Carmen having a heart attack. "But I think that's a small price to pay for doing what you love, no?"

I can only hope that the price stays small.

Chapter Three

When Thursday afternoon rolls around, I'm feeling one hundred percent more positive about my choice to join Atlético. Perhaps there was never anything negative about the opportunity to begin with, but I feel like I've been approaching life with a grain of salt lately. When you've found something precious and you've been through a lot to get it, it's hard not to eye things with an air of suspicion.

I am in the bedroom, slipping on a light blue silk Prada shirt when I hear Vera come inside the apartment. There is the sound of the lock rattling, the door closing, her shoes being kicked off, keys being placed on the table. It's a series of sounds that makes me feel safe.

Today, though, as I am getting dressed for my dinner later with Bon, a good friend I haven't seen in over a year, there is something different about Vera's entrance. There is a heaviness to the sounds, and when her shoe thumps on the floor, it lands hard.

"Vera?" I ask, tucking my shirt tails into my pants and coming out of the bedroom and down the hall. I stop by the entrance to the kitchen and living room. She is sitting on the arm of the couch, her head down, with peachy hair falling across her face, her hands in her lap. She looks defeated. For a moment I wonder if it's the heat that's dragging her down. Even with air conditioning, the place is muggy.

I gently place a hand on her shoulder. "Vera?"

She slowly looks up at me. She hasn't been crying—her eyes are dry—but her face looks extra pale and all the lipstick on her mouth has been bitten off.

"What's wrong?" I ask as I crouch down beside her, hands on her arm and thigh.

She sighs and her nose scrunches up slightly in embarrassment. "I think I'm getting fired."

"What?" I ask, obviously shocked. "Why? How? What happened?"

"I don't know," she says tiredly. "My boss, Patrice, pulled me in today and told me that my work visa for them will be up in September. She said she is unsure right now if they are going to apply for another one. There is another person who started last week, Amy, she's from Ireland and she speaks fluent Spanish. She only works once a week, but I think they are grooming her to take my place."

"That is ridiculous," I say, a path of warm rage making its way up my throat and clouding my words. "Why would they do that? You're perfect for the company. You make people feel welcome. I've seen you there, I know this. Your Spanish is coming along just fine too—they must see your improvements compared to when you started."

She shrugs like she's given up all hope. "I guess not. Patrice said something about the time it takes for the visa to go through—remember it took like a month or two last time—and that they are used to hiring people from the EU. Less paperwork."

I am beside myself. I straighten up and fold my arms, looking around the room as if it will give me answers. "Well, they cannot leave you hanging like this. Have you been officially let go?"

"No," she says. "Patrice said she'd let me know in a few weeks. I guess they are going to look into it a little bit more. I knew I should have been suspicious when the permit was only for six months to begin with. I don't know if they ever wanted me on more than a trial basis."

"But, Vera, you've been with them for almost a year now, it's just that some of that was under the table. They can't afford to, what would you say…yank your chain?"

"That or dick you around."

"They can't yank your dick or anything like that," I tell her, and start striding toward the door.

"Where are you going?" she quickly cries out, getting to her feet.

I grab my phone from the bowl on the counter and glance at it quickly before putting it in my pocket. "I'm going to go talk to Patrice."

"No, Mateo," she says, her bare feet scuffling over to me. She grabs hold of my arm and stares at me with pleading eyes. "Please don't. This isn't your problem."

I widen my eyes incredulously. "It isn't my problem? Yes it is, Vera. You are my lover, my friend, my everything. But you being here right now is dependent on them. I'm not letting them take that away from me."

She manages a sympathetic smile. "I know. But there are other ways. I'll get another job."

"When does the permit officially run out?"

"September 5th."

"You'll get another job in two weeks? I don't even know if it works that way. You can't just transfer a permit from one company to another."

She throws her hands up. "Then I'll work under the table for someone until they give me a new one."

I can't help but shake my head. I have a bad feeling in my gut, like someone has placed stones there. "It's risky. If you get caught, you'll be deported."

"Then I won't get caught."

I take hold of her hand. "You know I'd be more than happy to take care of you." I've told her this many times, how she doesn't have to work, that she can just do whatever she pleases and I'll take care of everything. It only seems to raise the hackles on her back.

"But I'd still be here illegally if you did," she says. "At least this way I have a chance. Anyway, maybe they won't let me go. I'll just work extra hard for them. I'll prove that I am better."

I admire her tenacity and can only hope it will be that easy. Still, I do want to talk to Patrice. But perhaps now, when I am heated up and likely to say things I will regret, it's not the best time. Las Palabras may have brought us together, but I will be damned if they are the ones to tear us apart.

"Do you want me to stay home tonight?" I ask her. "We could have some wine, go out to a movie?"

She rubs her lips together and quickly shakes her head. "No. You haven't seen this Bon fellow in forever. I'll just call Claudia and we'll go out somewhere. What kind of a name is Bon, anyway?"

"It's short for Bonaventure," I say. "His mother was French. And very strange. Used to powder her face with blue cornstarch, according to Bon." I grew up with Bon living down the street from me in Madrid, though these days he only comes back every now and then. The rest of the time he's a freelance photographer, usually for non-profit organizations that have him gallivanting in the rainforest or in remote villages.

"I really don't want to leave you like this," I tell her, pulling her into my chest and wrapping my arms around her. "I hate being given a problem that I can't immediately solve."

"I know," she mumbles into me. "Maybe when Monday rolls around, everything will right itself. I mean, you'll be starting your new job, maybe."

Maybe. I wasn't sure when I would actually start. But it didn't seem fair that the universe had this way of giving you one thing by taking away another. I knew it was the law of equilibrium and balance, but I didn't think it was asking too much for us both to have jobs we were happy about.

Or maybe it was.

I meet Bon at a tapas bar off of Plaza Mayor. The cobblestone streets are thick with tourists and drunk college students getting a head start on their weekend. I weave my way through them, unable to grab ahold of their enthusiasm. Vera's news has put a damper on everything and my brain has latched onto this worry, allowing it to grow unchecked.

I find him at the back, in a dark corner booth, munching on a bowl of almonds. Bon is probably around forty by now, a short man compared to me, but he has this way of making himself look taller. His mother had instilled proper posture in him as a small boy, and now, combined with the fact that he only wears all black, it makes all the difference.

"Bon," I say heartily, feeling a layer of anxiety slough off at his familiar face. His dark hair is thinning a bit on top but otherwise he looks the same.

He slides out of the booth and shakes my hand while I slap him affectionately on the back.

"Mateo," he greets me, "you haven't changed a bit." He pauses, eyes twinkling. "Or maybe you have. You seem lighter somehow."

I grab my stomach though I know my abs have never changed. "Eating better, I guess."

The twinkle amplifies and he smirks. "I bet you have. Come sit down."

He quickly waves over the waitress and orders us two beers. Bon has always been a talker, and I don't stop him while he launches into all the interesting things he's been doing over the last year and a half.

Finally, after three beers, the conversation slows and he eyes me impetuously. "Enough about me," he says. "How is Chloe Ann?"

Her name always makes me smile. "She is doing well. She will start going to school in September. She's rather excited about it."

"And Isabel?"

My face falls. "Surely you know we are divorced."

He nods and leans back in his seat. "I know. But I would like to hear it from you. We don't talk much anymore, Mateo, so I only know what I hear from other people. Or what I read in the newspapers online."

"I see." I stare at Bon, wondering what he'll say, if he'll understand. I am not sure if what he has seen and heard is anything different from the truth. I clear my throat. "Well, Isabel and I are divorced now. I met another woman."

"A younger woman. A Canadian."

"Yes," I tell him. "She is both those things and more than those things. Her name is Vera."

"She's got a hell of a lot of tattoos," he points out, as if he knows her. This bothers me.

"She does," I admit. "I happen to love them."

Bon laughs joylessly. "You, Mateo Casalles, with all your style and elegance, love a woman covered in tattoos. I would have thought it trashy to you."

"I would have thought this bar here to be trashy, yet here I am with you, Bon."

He lowers his head. "Are you trying to insult me?"

"Are you trying to insult me?"

He drains his beer. "Come, come, it is just an ob-servation, nothing more. I am curious. Who isn't? We all want to know about the woman who has made the great Mateo live a life of scandal and give up his beautiful, classy wife."

There is an edge to his words. Bon had never been a fan of Isabel, so I'm sure the news had originally delighted him. He leans forward, twirling his beer be-tween his hands. "Is it true that she's only twenty-three?"

I bristle, hating this gossip, hating that people know things about her from other sources. "She's twenty-four now."

"And you are nearly forty, yes? Quite the age dif-ference."

"Are you jealous?"

He shrugs. "Maybe. I'm not a fan of tattoos on women, though I've seen my share in different parts of the world. Tell me, Mateo, are you happy?"

"I've never been happier."

He appraises me carefully before taking another sip. I'm starting to get a bit of a headache. "You seem happy. I must say when I first heard of this, I didn't think it was true. I was going to ring you up but decided it was probably something I shouldn't concern myself with. If you want to go through an early mid-life crisis, it's not my business. It happens to every man."

"It is not a crisis," I grind out through my teeth.

"I can see that," he says, "and that's what I'm surprised about. You're still with her, yes?"

I can only nod. My heart is beginning to race.

"I must say I am surprised. Usually such a fling doesn't last."

"It was never a fling."

His mouth quirks up. "Oh, of course. You find some young pussy on your work excursion, fall into bed with her, your wife finds out and divorces you, but it was never a fling."

It takes all I have to prevent myself from slamming my fists on the table. "That's not how it happened."

"No?" he asks. "Do tell."

He's being an asshole and I can't figure out why. He always loved to push my buttons and rile me up, but this time it feels more personal. Maybe because for the first time, it is personal.

"I met Vera while I was in the language immersion program. I feel in love with her. Nothing happened…" And that isn't true, something did happen. I slept with her. I committed adultery, something I swore I would never do. But I feel too ashamed to admit this to him, not when I feel he will use it against me. "But I did realize that what I had with Isabel wasn't right, it wasn't what we wanted, and that the marriage was over. When Vera went back to Vancouver, I ended things."

"But Vera must have come back before your divorce was final."

I nodded. "Yes. Perhaps I was a bit impatient. But I couldn't stand to have her so far away from me."

"I don't blame you," he says. "I've seen the pictures. Even the topless ones. I couldn't leave those breasts."

My eyes narrow into hot slits. "If you say one more thing, don't you fucking think I won't reach across this table and strangle you."

"There's the old boy," he says with a laugh. "Hot-headed Mateo. I was wondering when he would come out."

"You better watch yourself," I warn him, unamused. I jab my finger at him. "I take Vera very seriously. That could be my future wife you're talking about."

His eyes widen in surprise and then cloud over with something akin to pity. "Oh dear. You can't be serious."

I wish I never said anything. It was something that had only been in my head, now it was in Lucia's, and now it was in Bon's.

"Mateo, Mateo, Mateo," Bon says with a sigh. "Stop holding on to your youth, old boy. This type of woman is good for a few rolls in the sack. Maybe many. She looks like she'd fuck you into another decade. It has done wonders for you, you look great. But that's all she is. That's all those types of girls are. Now what you should have done, was have your fun with her, and never told Isabel. Now you've got a divorce for nothing. You really think you can go and marry this Vera? You can't. Stop fooling yourself. The way you met, you know that kind of thing can't last. You should stop lying to yourself and let it be what it is."

I don't even know how to respond. All I know is that he's wrong. I know he's wrong. Then why do I feel that thread of doubt deep inside?

He continues, seemingly tired now. "I know you, Mateo. You always want to do the right thing. So noble sometimes that it's boring. That's why this little episode of yours has me interested, you see. It's not like you, not the you that I know. But now, you feel that because you threw out a perfectly acceptable marriage, you must hang on to this girl, make her, mold her, into something that she isn't. You need to learn to let go. You can't marry a tattooed, twenty-four-year-old Canadian girl. It won't work, and you'll be trapped in a world of unhappiness even worse than your first." He taps his hand on the table. "You need to start thinking less with your dick and more with your mind. Let her go and find someone else your own age, with your own class."

He gets up and excuses himself to the bathroom before I can say anything. Bon had once been my friend, but now I am not sure if that's true. This sounds like more than just concern. Has he been talking to Isabel? Is he jealous or just disapproving?

I don't know. But what I do know is that I don't need to listen to it.

I go up to the waitress and slip her a hundred euros to cover the bill. Then I leave the bar—and Bon—behind.

When I arrive back at the apartment, Vera isn't back yet. The long walk has done nothing to calm my nerves—in fact the heat seems to have only made it worse—so I pour myself a large glass of scotch that I save for rare occasions and sit outside on the balcony.

There is a slight breeze up here, and the hustle and bustle of the street below distracts me.

Bon is wrong. That's all there is to it. Though there is some truth. It's true that I have always tried to do the right thing—that is probably why I stuck with Isabel for so long—and that I care highly about reputation, whether it be my family's or my own.

But things change. Sometimes all it takes for a person to lose themselves is to find another. Perhaps it wasn't such a good thing, to always be noble, to have appearances be the first concern. Maybe it was what I needed, to find Vera, to let go of the person I had tried so hard to be, and just finally be myself.

I just wish it wasn't so hard.

I sit there for a long time, listening to people chatting on the street, the roar of cars as they zoom past. When the scotch starts to pull me under into the stickiness of sleep, I get up and head back inside just in time to see Vera stumble through the front door.

She's drunk, her breasts nearly spilling out of her low-cut dress, her hair half-up and half-down, wild around her face.

"Have fun?" I ask as she leans haphazardly against the counter and tries to kick off her slingbacks to no avail. "Hold on," I tell her gently, and crouch down beside her. She leans on me for support as I pull her shoes off and place them beside mine on the shoe rack underneath the coat hooks.

"Thanks, baby," she slurs, and I feel the weight of her on my back. I place my hands around the small of her waist and hold her steady as I straighten up. Her makeup is smudged and she's giving me a crooked smile.

"No problem," I tell her, peering at her closely. "Where did you guys go?"

She shrugs. "I don't really remember. We met up with Ricardo at some bar. He was there with a bunch of his friends."

A fist of unease opens in my stomach. I like Claudia's boyfriend Ricardo a lot, but the two times I've met his friends, they failed to impress me. They were young and brash with no scruples, like a bunch of modern-day Spaniards trying to resurrect Sid Vicious. I didn't like it when Vera went out with them, but then again, it's not like I would go. Bar hopping and clubbing weren't my scene anymore but they were definitely Vera's.

"I see," I say. "Sounds like you had a good time."

She shrugs. "Lots of shots and dancing. The usual." She attempts to take off her dress, and I help her out by pulling down the zipper. She's stark naked underneath but for once I have no interest in fucking her. My anxiety seems to build instead, and I'm staring at her body wondering why someone like me deserves it if I don't even have the desire to go out with her and her friends.

"Are you going to take me to bed?" she asks, batting her eyes and biting her lip.

Naturally, I will take her but not in the way she thinks, not when she is this drunk. I've learned my lesson a few times before.

Sure enough, the moment she climbs into the sheets and lays her head back onto the pillow, she closes her eyes and passes out. Light snoring ensues.

I sigh and tuck her in, then fill up a glass of water for her and get out two ibuprofen. She never does very well in the mornings after a night of drinking, and since she still has work at Las Palabras in the morning, she needs to be on her best behavior.

I strip down to nothing and get in bed as well. She's not the only one with a big day ahead of her. Tomorrow, everything changes.

Yet, it feels like everything has already changed.

Chapter Four

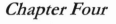

Friday and the weekend rolled on by almost as usual. There was, of course, the event of me calling Pedro and informing him that I would be delighted to take the position. I celebrated that by having a bit of brandy in my coffee. Vera was at work, terribly hung over, otherwise she would have partaken in the moment.

Saturday we picked up Chloe Ann and took her to an outdoor children's concert. She was a bit moodier than normal, perhaps because the heat never relented, but she seemed to enjoy herself by the end of it. Cotton candy fixes all of life's problems when you're a child.

Sunday was a day of lazing around, reading the paper and drinking drunken lemonade. It was easy to fool ourselves into thinking everything was fine.

But today, I know things aren't fine. I feel it when I wake up, that gnawing sensation of something eating away at me. I should be happy, on cloud nine—I'm about to get dressed and head into the office at the stadium, to start my first official day at a job I'd even dreamed of when I was back on the team.

And yet my gut is a ball of nerves.

Even Vera senses it as we shower together; her brows knit together in a mix of discomfort and concern.

"Are you all right?" she asks. "You seem distant."

"Like I'm in another galaxy?" I answer, turning her around to rub soap on her back.

She lifts her hair off her shoulders to give me access. "Something like that."

"I guess I'm nervous about my first day," I tell her.

She nods. "I'm nervous this will be my last."

I pause, and she shoots me an apologetic look over her shoulder. "I'm sorry, I know it's not about me."

"Maybe it's always about you," I whisper. "I can't pretend that I'm not afraid for us."

Her face falls slightly. "Don't worry," she says, and I almost believe that she doesn't. "I worked my ass off on Friday. They won't let me go. I won't let them."

I lean down and kiss her shoulders, tasting the soap and the freshness of her skin. "You can do anything you put your mind to. But it doesn't mean I won't worry."

She turns around, her eyes determined. "You know that we'll be okay, don't you? This will all work out. It's just a hiccup, that's all."

I try and give her a smile but it fails to form on my lips. "I'm just tired of the universe giving me something and taking something else away."

"Well, the universe can go fuck itself for all I care," she says. "You deserve this job. I deserve mine. There's no reason why we can't have both."

She's right. There is no reason. But maybe I'm still afraid that we got off too easy, that there is still punishment for our actions. Bon reminded me that though the ink on the divorce papers is dry, the wounds are still fresh for everyone involved.

I still have that thought on my mind as I drive to work, to the stadium by the river. I haven't been back here in years, not even to watch a game. It feels strange but still right at the same time.

As most first days are, this one is easy. I don't even meet the team, just the administrative staff, plus Diego and Warren. Even though I expected contempt from Warren for taking over what should have been his job, he's friendly enough, and Diego is as cordial as the first time I met him, if not a little defensive over the team. I don't blame him. Even though his eyes and heart are set on Argentina, he is the guy that helped bring this team back. It's personal to him so I treat him and his views with respect.

At the end of the day, after I am shown a small desk in the same room as Warren's where I am to temporarily work, Pedro calls me into his office. He's sitting behind a Lucite table with a wooden cigar box in his hands. His walls are white and covered with rich black and white photographs of the team; his windows are large and wide and look out onto the grassy field and the rows of seats in the stadium.

"Sit down," he commands, and I do so in a plastic chair that is so modern it's uncomfortable. He opens the cigar box, sticks one in his mouth, and then tilts it toward me in offering.

I raise my hand, shaking it off. I make a point of not smoking cigars with people I don't know that well—I hate the idea of being stuck with someone while you're waiting for the paper to burn.

"Suit yourself," he mumbles out of the corner of his mouth, then lights one up. He puffs on it for a few moments, his grey brows furrowed in concentration until he has it burning just the right way. "How was your first day?" he asks when he's finally satisfied.

"Very good," I said. "Diego has been very welcoming and Warren seems to be easy to get along with."

"He is, he is," he says with a nod. "Just too bad he's not a Spaniard. Though what's too bad for him is great for you."

I smile placidly at him, feeling like there is a more serious undertone to this conversation other than checking in on me.

He continues, "This, of course, will be a slow start for you. But I think that is for the best. It's good for you to just observe for the next few months. I believe you can learn a lot more by watching and listening than by doing."

"I agree."

"Good," he says, leaning forward slightly. "But even though we will ease you into things, the moment you signed the contracts this morning is the moment you became part of the team, part of this administration, this international symbol of Spain."

I nod. Uh-huh.

"And as part of this team, you have a certain reputation to uphold. Now, your personal life is none of my business. In fact, if it weren't for your face showing up in the tabloids late last year, we might have forgotten all about you. Though I am sure it was not intentional, it did help. But now that you are here, I do think there needs to be an air of . . . respect and class when it comes to representing Atlético. Do you agree?"

I think I say yes. I can barely tell, the blood is whooshing so loudly in my head. I am braced for something horrible and I don't know what it is.

"As I said," he goes on, "your personal life is none of my business. But if you could, I would prefer it not to appear in the papers anymore."

I frown. "It hasn't."

He gives me a sharp smile. "Oh, but it has. Don't you read them, Mateo? Perhaps you should."

Pedro reaches into his drawer and pulls out a copy of Diez Minutos, my most hated magazine. Cheap, tawdry, and tacky, it was the first one to spread lies about me and Vera, and I immediately think back to the photographer I saw taking my picture outside of Fioris over a week ago. But how could a picture of me, leaving the restaurant alone, spark any sort of concern from Pedro?

He shows me. He flips a few pages, and there I see a fuzzy photograph of Vera. She is wearing the same sexy clothes she was wearing on Thursday night. She is dancing close with a man that is not me, and laughing.

I think I'm going to be sick. I do what I can to keep my face as neutral as possible, and I look up to him as I say, "So, that is Vera. What about it?"

But I know what the problem is because it's a problem for me too. I don't want to examine the photos any closer, not with him watching me, waiting for a reaction that I refuse to give him.

"Have you read the headline?" he asks, jabbing a finger at it. I hadn't. I glance at it now, quickly.

Mateo Casalles Has New Competition.

I swallow and look up at Pedro. "All lies," I say.

"If you read it," Pedro says, "it goes on to say that your girlfriend was seen partying at a local hotspot last Thursday night and getting close with a young man. It then goes on to say that there are rumors of you joining Atlético in a managerial position. How could one be true and the other not?"

I shift my jaw back and forth for a moment, trying to quell the embarrassment and rage that threatens to shatter me. "Do you not remember the photographer standing outside of the restaurant after our last meeting?

It would be easy for him to deduce that I am involved in Atlético again."

"Stupid paparazzi," he mutters, though I'm tempted to point out that it was him who waved for the camera.

"Yes," I say, making a motion to get up and leave, "they are stupid. They made assumptions about me which turn out to be half true—coaching is not exactly a managerial position. They make assumptions about Vera, that this boy she is dancing with is someone more than a friend. Their whole business is based on selling assumptions. Everyone knows that."

"It looks bad, Mateo," Pedro says as I stand up. "This was normal when you were younger, and it's normal for the players, especially a few particular ones, but I don't want to see this from their coach. You might need to put your girlfriend on a leash if she can't behave."

I raise my brows. "Excuse me?" My voice is hard and cold.

Pedro looks mildly apologetic. "Sorry. I don't mean to insult her, or you, but I just want you to be aware of your image now going forward. You don't work for yourself anymore. The restaurant is long gone. You work for me, for Atlético, for Madrid. You have a face to show the public. Preserve it."

I can only nod in response before I turn and leave the room. Somehow I manage to keep it together until I can't handle it anymore. I pull over beside a newsstand to quickly snap up a copy. I read it over when I'm in my building's parking garage.

Up close, the pictures are worse. There are two of them. In both they are dancing; in one Vera is laughing and the boy leans in close. In the other, he has his hands around her waist. From the fuzzy details I can make out that he is one of Ricardo's friends—spiked hair, leather, studs, and tattoos. He looks like someone that Vera would be with. He looks like the opposite of me.

I fight the urge to rip the magazine in half, to pound my head against the steering wheel, to find Claudia then find Ricardo, and punch his face in just by association. I zero in on his hands, the possessive way he is holding her, and I think I may just lose my mind.

She is mine, not his. Why is she letting this happen?

I swallow hard and try to breathe through my anger. It's an uphill battle. I tell myself that the photos don't mean anything. It doesn't mean Vera is having an affair. It doesn't mean that she's sleeping with this guy, that she's in love with him. It doesn't mean they are a better match. For all I know, he may have made her laugh, put his hands on her, and in the next moment got a drink in his face. Vera is feisty like that, too. The photographs don't tell the whole story.

There is only one way to find out. I have to confront her, immediately, before I make this bigger than it actually is. My mind is always eager to make things worse. I shove the magazine in my suit jacket pocket and take the excruciatingly slow elevator up to our floor. It's four in the afternoon and she should be home.

At the door, I pause, trying to go over how I'll approach her. Vera can get very defensive over things, whether she's guilty of them or not, and the last thing I need is a fight because she's mad that I'm mad. Funny how it usually works out that way.

I suck in my breath and open the door. She is on the balcony, stirring a large iced coffee from Starbucks, reading a hardcover book in the shade. For a moment I think I should leave her alone in peace, but then I know I won't get any peace that way.

"Hey, handsome," she says, pulling her oversized sunglasses away from her eyes and glancing up at me as I stand in the doorway. "How was your first day?"

When I don't come any closer, her eyes trail to the magazine poking out from my jacket. I can tell she hasn't seen it before. She looks curious but not ashamed.

"It was fine," I say. I try to smile, but from the way her brows knit together, I can tell that it reads false.

"Are you doing some light reading?" she asks, eyes back to the magazine.

"Tell me again about Thursday night."

She pushes her sunglasses to the top of her head. There is a smattering of new freckles across her nose. She must have gotten some sun during her lunch hour. It's cute, but I push aside my affections for now.

"Thursday night?"

"Yes, Vera. You went out with Claudia. You came back drunk. Where did you go? Who was there? What did you do?"

She blinks and then rubs at her forehead. "I told you. I don't know, it was the usual. We went to some place near the university, I don't remember the name. Something Spanish, obviously. We drank and danced and did shots."

"Who was there?"

She frowns. "Claudia. Ricardo. His friends."

"Are his friends your friends?"

"Sure, why not?"

"Any of them stand out to you in particular?"

"Mateo . . . what are you talking about? What's going on?"

I shrug. "I don't know, Vera. I would like some answers though." I take the magazine and toss it on the table. "Flip a few pages in and give them to me."

She stares at me for a few moments, and now she's worried. She bites her lip and turns the magazine over, flipping through it. The page is already worn and wrinkled from my hands and comes easily to her.

She gasps, her hand shaking near her mouth. "What the fuck?" she whispers as she stares down at it with the same kind of horror that I had.

"Yes. What the fuck."

She slowly looks at me. "Mateo, you can't . . . this is Paulo, one of Ricardo's good friends. You've met him. I don't . . . I was just dancing with him."

I stay silent. It has the most power.

Her expression has turned from confused to pleading. "Are you mad over this?"

My eyes burn into hers. "Am I mad? I'm a bit mad, Vera. A bit upset. A bit confused. And a lot embarrassed. Do you know how I found this out? Because my new boss, Pedro del Torro, owner of Atlético, showed it to me, telling me that my girlfriend was going after other men, and it was making the news."

She stands up, her face growing red, and throws her arms out to the side. "Well, what the hell am I supposed to do? Not go out, ever? Not dance, ever?"

"Why is he touching you like this? Why are you with him like this?"

She shakes her head frantically. "No, no, no. Mateo, it's not what you think."

I wish my heart would stop beating so fast, so loud, like it's teetering on the edge. "Then tell me what I think and tell me how I'm wrong. Please."

She walks around to me and reaches out for my arm. Her grip is tight and desperate. I want so badly to believe whatever will come out of her mouth. "I was just dancing with Ricardo's friend. He's my friend too, I guess. He's touchy-feely, but then again, so are you."

That was the wrong thing to say and she knows it. Her lips clamp shut for a moment and she looks panicked.

"I am this touchy-feely with you because you are mine to touch," I say, trying to keep my voice measured and steady. "Not his. Not anyone else's."

Her eyes widen momentarily. "Mateo, you can't get mad because someone touches me."

I match her look. I'm not sure I can believe what she's saying. "Of course I can get mad. I have the right to."

"Well, where I come from, things like that don't mean anything."

"Where you come from is very different from here, with people different from me. You made me look like a fucking fool, Vera."

The ferocity in my words catch both of us off-guard. "I didn't know someone would take my picture," she says.

"So the only problem," I say, "is that you got caught?"

"I didn't do anything!" she cries out, angry now, all curled fists and blazing eyes. "It was just a fucking dance. What the hell are you so bothered about then, is it that everyone is reading this shit and believing it, or that I go out and have fun without you, that other men happen to find me attractive?"

I blink and raise my hands, stunned. "Whoa, whoa, what are you talking about? Why is this something *you're* angry about?"

"I'm angry," she says, "because you treat me like property sometimes."

I am aghast. My heart lurches uncomfortably in my chest, and I only now realize we are having a very loud argument outside on the balcony.

"You are my property," I tell her, completely genuine. It's not exactly what I mean to say – it's her heart and soul I wish to own – but it's the closest word in translation to me. It doesn't go over well with her.

"You're a caveman."

I smile coldly. "Cavemen fall in love, too."

"Well, I don't like it," she sneers, folding her arms.

"And I don't like that you don't seem to have any respect for me," I retort, then remember to lower my voice. It doesn't matter, it looks like I've slapped her across the face.

"No respect?" she whispers raggedly.

"Hanging off of other men, going out, getting drunk," I go on.

"First of all, I am not hanging off of other men," she says, pointing her finger in the air. "That was a picture taken at the wrong time."

I both bite my tongue and raise my brow.

"Second of all, going out, getting drunk? That's just what I do. That has nothing to do with respect for you, Mateo. I find those things fun. Jesus Christ, you think you can just lock me up in your apartment and swill scotch all night, or maybe take me to your parents or to some of your so-called friends who look at me like I'm nothing but a slutty homewrecker, and who are boring as fuck? It's not my fault that I'm still young and you're not anymore."

Now it feels like I'm the one who has been hit. Not a slap, but a wrecking ball right into my chest.

Vera sees it. Her face falls slightly, torn between wanting to battle and wanting to sympathize. "I'm sorry," she says quickly, "I didn't mean it like that."

"You meant it enough to say it," I say quietly, tearing my eyes away from her. The irony is that Vera is always the one telling me that I'm not old, that I'm still in my thirties, that when I hit forty the forties are the new thirties. But how could she even know that? It'll be another six years before she's even thirty. We're on totally different wavelengths.

I thought she'd found herself when she found me. Now I am not so sure.

"We both say things we don't mean when we're angry," she explains.

I still avoid her eyes. "And why again are *you* angry?"

"Because I don't like having to defend myself against something I shouldn't. I don't like feeling guilty for trying to live my life the only way I know how. It's like the only time we're really together, really a couple is when we're both here. Other than that, our lives don't mesh at all, and whatever way I'm living it is all completely wrong to you."

I don't like the tone her voice is taking, full of regret and resignation, of months of things unsaid. It makes me bleed, undoes me, to think that all this time she's been suffering her days in some way or another, keeping her true feelings to herself.

"So what are you saying?" I ask her, my voice surprisingly level. "That you're only mine when you're here?" I glance at her, and she's flicking her fingers against each other, leaning from one foot to the other. "And out there you're free to belong to whoever?"

She stares at me for a few moments, still fidgeting. "I always belong to myself."

"And to me second . . ." I rub my hand along the back of my neck and feel only sweat and heat. It's getting too hard to breathe anywhere. The month is suffocating us.

"I can belong to both of us at the same time," she says, though it sounds like she's conceding. I watch her carefully. Her shoulders seem to relax a touch.

"Just promise me you'll watch yourself," I say warily.

She shoots daggers at me, back on the defensive. "I'm not fucking twelve years old."

I roll my eyes. "I'm not saying you are a child, Vera. I'm saying just have some respect for me when you're out there, and this will all be over. We won't have to discuss this again."

"No, it won't be over," she says. "Because I do have respect for you. I'm fucking in love with you, you big idiot."

Her words don't have their intended effect. I turn suddenly and snatch the magazine up from the table, shoving it in her face. "This is not a picture of woman who is in love with me. This is a picture of . . ." And she is right in that we say things we don't mean when we are angry. I at least manage to hold my words in. But she can see right through me in that uncanny way of hers.

Her pupils are shocked into pinpricks. "A drunken whore, that's what you were going to say."

I was not going to say that, not exactly. My thoughts had been more polite, but that was close.

"There is a difference," I say carefully, "between being something and acting like something."

"Is there?" she asks. "Because you're being a chauvinistic asshole right now and acting like it, too."

"Why don't you call me old again, or is there no venom left in you?"

"Oh, there is plenty of venom."

I step over to her until she's backed against the table. She looks unnerved for a moment until I grab her hand and press it to my heart. I peer down at her, my gaze unwavering.

"This is me. This is who I am. You knew that when you met me." I lean in closer until I feel submerged in the gold flecks of her eyes. "You know the things I care about. Pride, yes. Respect. For me. For family. For relationships. If these things cause me to be, what did you say, a *chauvinistic asshole*, then it can't be of any surprise to you."

There's something about the way she's staring up at me—feral and subtly violent, like a cornered wolf—that's turning me on. The heat is no longer just the thick dusty air or the sweat on my skin, or the anger simmering in my heart—it's a warm tidal wave pushing through the center of me. Before I know it, I'm hard and my breathing has become heavier.

It does nothing to temper the wildness in her eyes. It doesn't have to.

"You surprise me each day," she says, voice flinty but drawn-out. Her gaze drops to my mouth.

The pressure inside me builds, my eyelids becoming leaden. I put my hand to the back of her neck and grip her there. She's infuriating me, this inability of hers to understand how I feel. Sometimes I feel she has less at stake in our relationship than I do, though I know that's not always true.

"You need to understand that you're mine," I tell her. It comes out more as a hiss now, and my lips are at her ear, inches away from the moisture of her skin. "Only I can do this to you. No one else. Not anyone else."

I reach down and unzip my fly. She stiffens slightly at the action, and I pause, letting her reactions cue me. She relaxes, and that's all I need to lift her up and place her ass on the edge of the wrought iron table. It teeters a bit under her weight, but it holds.

Her eyes are now a mix of lust and fight. She's still angry, still ready to battle. So am I. But it's coming out in a different way now. I don't normally associate anger with sex, so this is new to me. As I stare into her eyes, slipping my hand between her skirt and legs to push her underwear aside, I can see it surprises her too. I guess I do surprise her every day.

"This doesn't fix things," she says defiantly, but she's wrapping her legs around me as she says it, tugging me toward her. The table wobbles.

"How do you know?" I whisper, and simultaneously guide my cock toward her while laying my lips and teeth on the side of her neck. At the moment, I feel like it might fix things for me. I feel like I could drive all other men out of her, make myself permanent in her temporary world. We are outside, within earshot of neighbors who just need to peek around the partition to see us; we are in plain view of any apartments across the street.

I wish the photographer was there, taking a photo of this. I'd show them who she really belonged with. I'd show them I am up to the task.

I push myself into her. She gasps, her face laced with pain. She is not wet enough for me, and though the pleasure that radiates through me from my balls to my neck feels like nothing else, I hesitate, about to pull out. I want this rough and fast and hard, but I will not make her suffer.

But she tightens her legs around my hips and holds me to her possessively. I go in slower this time, my lips back at her neck, wanting to make a mark. I bite and nibble and suck the blood to the surface. My thrusts now are sharp and deliberate. The table rocks noisily, and her breathless gasps turn to breathless moans.

It feels impossible to shed the fire burning inside me yet I try, faster, harder, more desperate, more angry, more lost. In the heat of day, I am wet to the touch, and she is tight around me, and the air feels like a damp wool blanket; it only fuels the madness.

She is mine, she is mine, she is mine.

I am hers.

Even in this simmering frustration, I remember to be a gentleman. I slide my fingers between her legs with one hand while I hold the back of her neck with the other. The minute that I feel her tense, her breath catching in her throat, I let myself go inside her. I am straining, holding on to her, not caring that my own cries are soaring over the busy street below.

We are both breathing heavily, and I pull back to look at her. She's drowsy with sex, but there is something still rebellious in her eyes. Though my body is relieved from coming, my heart is not. I pull out of her, zip up my fly, and help her off the edge of the table. Then I turn away, confused. She was right—it didn't fix anything.

I leave her there on the balcony and walk into the house. Out of habit, I check to make sure my wallet is in my pants, and grab my keys.

"Where are you going?" she asks after me. She sounds hardened but slightly panicked.

"I need to clear my head," I tell her, and leave, shutting the door behind me.

Of course, there is no place for me to go. Vera has Claudia and the people she works with. I don't have anyone. Maybe my parents, my sister. Every other friend I had I lost when I left Isabel. Even the great friends turned out not to be so great, and subtly distanced themselves from me, perhaps afraid of being sucked into a scandal, perhaps worried that my behavior would rub off on them. I'm sure many of their wives had been behind it, threatening their husbands that if they should ever hang out with a man who would toss aside his wife for a younger girl, they might do the same.

I had so many friends that I'd lost just because they didn't want to understand what it was like to fall in love with someone you're not supposed to. So many friends who chose to judge me than to love me.

I go out into the streets instead, walking and walking until the sun sets, and I find a small, quiet bar to have a drink at. I order a gin and tonic to deal with the heat, extra gin to deal with my heart. Everything weighs so heavy right now, I can feel it pressing down on my shoulders. There is Vera, and then there is loneliness. Sometimes I have both but now it only feels like I have the latter.

I want so badly to read over my letter, but that is back at the apartment with her, and I am here. She hasn't texted me—there are no "where are yous?" and "when are you coming backs?" or "we need to talks," or even "chauvinistic assholes"—so I feel no urge to return. I want to stay out on the streets of Madrid until the sun comes up. I want to drink and walk down narrow streets filled with dubious people until I feel like I have an answer to the buried question that is plaguing me.

Can you adapt to something without changing? Can you give without losing all of yourself?

I am not sure.

Eventually though, my feet hurt—my work shoes are brand new and not meant to broken in in one go—and my bones are tired. It must come with old age.

I trek back to the apartment and enter as quietly as possible. It is dark and silent excerpt for the hum of the fridge.

Vera is in bed but she is not asleep. She is sitting up, her shoulders slumped forward, and wearing one of my t-shirts. The curtain is open and the light spills in, illuminating one side of her and leaving the rest in shadow. Her cheeks glisten. She has been crying.

"I'm sorry," she whispers as I stand in the doorway. All at once, my anger is gone, replaced with nothing but love for this scared little girl.

I come over to the bed and pull her into my arms. I kiss the top of her head as hard as I can. "I am sorry."

"I'm just being stubborn," she sniffles into me. "I don't know why. I guess I'm afraid, and I'm frustrated, and I feel so, so *trapped*."

I stiffen. "Trapped?"

"Not by you," she says adamantly. "Never you. It's . . . I don't know my place here yet and I feel like everywhere I turn there is just something trying to push me away. I don't belong in Vancouver, and yet I don't feel like I belong here either."

"You belong with me," I tell her, my voice raw with passion, with longing.

"I know," she says, nodding, "I know I do. But sometimes that isn't enough. I need more than just you, Mateo. I need you, and I need a life of my own that I feel secure in. I need a place to plant my roots."

"Can't that be here?"

"I hope so. I'm just afraid that Spain doesn't want me to stay."

I run my hand down the back of her head. "I will talk to your boss. You will be able to stay."

"Mateo, that's okay." She says even though it's not, even though I will do whatever I can.

Yet as I kiss her, bury myself inside her, fall asleep with her, I'm only left with more questions.

Chapter Five

By the end of the week, I've settled nicely into my new position. Not being a coach at this point, just an observer, comes easily. The players are elated with me, which will make things smoother in the long run. At least, it will be smoother until I actually step up to the plate in January. I am sure once I am bossing them around, their attitudes will change. I already knew before I even went into this gig who was going to need the most work and who was going to be the most trouble. Thankfully, they aren't the same player.

Thursday night I go out for dinner with Vera, Claudia, and Ricardo. I know Vera is making an effort to include me in her other life, and I make an effort to be a part of it. It's a bit awkward though, sitting across the table from Ricardo when all I can think about is his derelict friend. Luckily, no one brings up the picture in the magazine, though I know by now everyone has seen it.

When we leave the restaurant though, late and tipsy on three bottles of grenache, flashbulbs go off in our faces. There are two photographers this time—it is now public news that I am Diego's replacement—and though my first instinct is to shield Vera and give the paparazzi the finger, I decide to take a moment and set things right.

I put my arm around Vera's waist and pull her into me, smiling broadly for the cameras. They loved my smile back in the day, they should still love it now.

"Nice to see you back together," one of the photographers, the bothersome one with the mullet, says.

"We were never apart," I answer smoothly before escorting her down the steps and toward Claudia and Ricardo, who are standing startled and bug-eyed on the sidewalk.

"Who were you with last week, Vera?" he asks.

I narrow my eyes briefly before I answer for her. "She's allowed to have friends, isn't she? Good evening, gentlemen." I raise my hand dismissively at them then nod at Claudia and Ricardo to keep walking. The four of

us quickly disappear down the street and out of the photographers' sight.

"Jesus," Claudia swears, brushing her long dark
hair behind her ears. "You're a celebrity all over again."

I shrug. "I guess now that I'm the future coach
they're all over it. Slow news month, perhaps." I squeeze
Vera's waist, both in support and as a reminder.

The next day, the photo of Vera and me has made
the online version of the magazine. Perhaps the two of us
looking happy together isn't as print-worthy as Vera
dancing with some punk, but it's still there. I don't know
who is out there reading it and getting false assumptions
about our life together, but I hope whoever they are, that
they see it. It's petty, perhaps, to care so much about what
thousands of strangers think, but that doesn't change the
fact that I do.

If Pedro has seen it, he doesn't mention it, and
when work is over I have a quick cigar with him while
walking the playing field. He's at least someone I can tolerate now for the length of a stogie. After that, when I
know that Vera has gone home for the day, I drive to the
Las Palabras office.

I haven't been here since I first boarded that bus last April, but it all comes back to me like it was only yesterday.

I remember being excited for the first time in a long time. The feeling was strange, to *feel* was strange. My nerves were jangled, and when I got on the bus I was embarrassed because all these strange faces were looking up at me, and I had to be the last person getting on, holding everything up. But, as I made my way down the aisle and found a pair of empty seats, and we still weren't taking off, I relaxed. I wasn't the last one.

I hadn't meant to be late, it was Isabel who was being deliberately slow, like she wanted me to miss the trip. She hadn't wanted me to go, thought there was no point in improving my English since I knew enough already. But that wasn't really the point. Good enough was never good enough for me, not when *better* was so easy to reach.

She took her time trying to find the place, despite me barking directions, and when she dropped me off at the office, she was more huffy than sad about my departure.

Sometimes I wonder what would have happened if she hadn't been that way, if I had gotten to the Las

Palabras office early. I would have gotten on the bus with everyone else. I would have sat next to maybe Ricardo or Jose Carlos or Nerea.

I would have never seen Vera get on the bus and sit beside me. I would have never felt every inch of my skin buzz as if shocked awake and watched her walk down the aisle, looking flushed and sexy and tattooed and young and impossibly, impossibly pretty. I would have never turned my staring eyes away from her and looked out the window as if I hadn't noticed her at all.

I would have never waited a few moments, composing myself, trying to find my English and my voice before turning to her, meeting her vibrant gaze and quirky, unsure lips to say, "Hello, I'm Mateo."

That was all it took for me, really. I shook her hand and felt this surge deep within my heart, like something was being unearthed after a very long time. There was no turning back. Back then I knew she was trouble, I was in trouble, and the rest of my life would be different. I didn't realize how different, but I knew then it couldn't stay the same. You don't keep your eyes on the ground once you've seen the beauty of the stars.

I let the memories fold over me, and I hold them close as I approach the office. The sign is flipped to

CLOSED but I can see a light on through the glass and the shadow of someone walking past. I rap my knuckles loudly on the door and wait.

A few moments pass, and there is movement on the other side of the door. I see a pair of cat-eyed glasses peer at me, and then something unlocks and the door opens.

"Mr. Casalles," Patrice says, looking me up and down. I've only met her once since she took over as manager at Las Palabras, at a small party, and she looks exactly the same. Close-cropped hair, sharp nose, sharp eyes under even sharper glasses.

"Call me Mateo, please," I tell her with my most charming smile.

She nods, birdlike. "Of course, Mateo. Come on in."

She gestures and I walk into the small office. It's a mess and I can tell where Vera sits because that section is even messier. There is a small arsenal of lipsticks scattered beneath the computer monitor and two seemingly empty cans of Diet Coke.

"I suppose you've come here to discuss Vera's situation," Patrice says, leaning against the door to what I presume is her private office.

I nod and am hit with this unnerving feeling like I'm at a parent-teacher meeting or something of that sort. "She doesn't know I'm here, of course," I quickly say to offshoot the idea. "And she'll hate me if she finds out. But I just wanted to get the real story from you. Sometimes I think she's protecting me a bit by not telling me everything."

That's not exactly true. I think Vera has been honest from the start, but Patrice doesn't have to know that.

She offers me a tense smile. "Very well. The thing is, Mateo, we're going to have to let Vera go."

I stare at her dumbly because I don't think I've heard her correctly. "I'm sorry?"

She sighs and wrings her hands, looking at the posters of happy as shit Spaniards on the wall. If I have heard correctly, I'm about to resent every single thing about this bastard company.

"We only got the six-month working visa for Vera because we just weren't sure if hiring her in the long-term was feasible. For one, she doesn't speak Spanish."

I glare at her. "She's learning. She's trying." My words are as sharp as her face.

"And that's good. But it's not good enough. We are a Spanish company and need someone who speaks both Spanish and English fluently."

"But she's just an administrator."

"Yes, but for how long? You of all people should know about growth and progress. What happens if our booking agent leaves? Vera would take her place. She cannot take her place with the way she is. Face it, she's not cut out for this job. She should, I don't know, be at a music store selling CDs."

"Those don't exist anymore," I say through grinding teeth.

She folds her arms crossly. "I know she's your . . . whatever she is to you, but you know what I mean. More than that, this job doesn't interest her. It's just a job. She won't make it her career and we won't either. Now, we already have someone who has just started helping out. She's part of the EU, there's no paperwork or legalities, no dealing with the government, and she's fluent in Spanish. It's just a better match for everyone."

There is no air left in my lungs, but I manage to say, "Everyone but Vera."

"I am sorry, Mateo," she says, and she does sound a bit sorry. But not sorry enough.

"Does she know?"

She shakes her head. "I was going to tell her on Monday and let her work that last week."

"You realize what's going to happen to her if you do this," I say, running a hand through my hair. The office is starting to feel so small. I stare at Vera's lipsticks on the desk, imagine her lips, and I feel something inside me coming undone. This can't be happening.

Her pointy eyebrows draw together and up. "Again, I am sorry, Mateo. I like Vera. She's a funny girl and very . . . sweet. But she doesn't belong here."

I have nothing more to say to Patrice. It's evident that even if I flashed my wallet at her, insinuated that Las Palabras could use donations for new office equipment, she wouldn't go for it. I leave and climb back into my SUV, spending a moment to think about what I should do. I have to do something. I have to think. If I don't, I will think about the inevitable. I will fall apart.

I am not used to being a man without a solution. When I fell in love with Vera, the solution was clear. I had to leave Isabel. It wasn't easy, but it was clear. Now, I have no solution and nothing is clear.

Vera doesn't have to work. I can easily support her. But she wants to work, and in order to stay in the country legally, she must work. There is always the option of university, but she had told me the foreign student fees were far beyond what she or her parents could afford—or would want to give—and she was adamant that though she was a good student, she wasn't good enough to qualify for any kind of aid. They would give her that in her own country for a Canadian school, but not here.

I had brought up the university option before, telling her I could pay for it, but she waved it off like it was just a dream. She wouldn't let me pay for it, and our back and forth about it turned into a fight.

Now I wonder if I can convince her again, now that deportation is on the line. It is probably too late for her to join the school year next month, but there is always the January semester. The only problem is that she would be illegal until then.

Maybe it won't be a big deal. There are thousands of illegal immigrants from Somalia, Nigeria, Mexico, El Salvador, all working under the table in Spain. They don't get caught. Vera doesn't have to either. If we play everything right, we might actually be able to ride this thing out.

Clinging to that thought like a lifeline, I speed back to the apartment, eager to cement this idea down.

Vera isn't home when I get in which only compounds my anxiety. Luckily by the time I've poured myself a scotch and settled uneasily on the couch, she appears in the front door, holding a small bag of groceries.

"Hola," she says brightly. "We were out of food and I was *staaaaarving*."

She plunks the bag on the counter and then comes over to give me a kiss. She seems to be in a good mood. I feel terrible that I'm about to ruin it for her.

"What's wrong?" she asks, staring at me with wide eyes. "I can feel it rolling off of you. What happened?"

I lick the scotch off my lips and sit back on the couch, holding her gaze steadily. "Remember what you said the other day, how everything was going to be okay?"

Her face blanches, turning paler than milk.

"Well," I continue, "keep that in mind. That it will be. Everything will be okay. I already have a solution."

"Mateo . . ."

"I went by Las Palabras today. Just now. After work."

She stares at me in horror. "No."

"Yes," I say. "I did. I wanted to talk to Patrice myself, figure out if there was something I could do, if we could come to some sort of arrangement."

"Mateo," she whines. "Oh god, what did you do?"

I give her a sad smile and shake my head. "I didn't do anything. It was too late, Vera. You were right, about the Irish girl who speaks Spanish. Patrice is planning on letting you go. She's telling you on Monday. Next week will be your last."

Her mouth forms a pretty little *O* shape and I immediately think of the lipsticks on her desk. I know why the sight had struck such a chord with me. Those lipsticks were such a small part of her, trying to fit in to the office, the world around her, and failing.

"I'm sorry," I say, and I really, truly, deeply am. I think she has no idea. "I tried but . . . she wouldn't have any of it. Her mind is set."

"Well," she says, straightening up, one hand on her hip, the other at her mouth, rubbing her fingers across it. "Like fuck I'll be staying for a week. Fuck the pay and fuck her. Fuck that whole program."

"Even though it's how we met?"

"What good is it if it lets us meet but won't let us stay?"

"I agree," I say. "Besides, she wasn't in charge at that time anyway. It doesn't count."

She plops down on the couch beside me and leans her head against my shoulder. I can feel her whole weight on me, and I know she's putting it in my hands. I am only too eager to handle it for her, I just hope I know how to get us out of it.

"What the hell am I going to do?" she asks, voice tired now.

"You're going to live here illegally until January. Then you'll go to school."

"What?"

"It's the only way. But it's not so hard, Vera. You'll see."

She sits up and eyes me incredulously. "It's not so hard? How do you know? Do you normally harbor illegal immigrants?"

I give her a half-smile. "I would if they all looked like you."

"This isn't funny."

I sigh. "No, it's not. But honestly, it's our best chance. It will have to do, anyway. Even if you go and find another job and convince them to sponsor you, that will take some time, so it will have to be this way. It just has to."

"And what were you talking about with the whole school thing?"

"Your astronomy degree. There is no reason why you can't finish it at the universities here."

"Uh, yes there is. It's called money. I don't have that."

"But I do."

"Mateo, we've been over this. I don't want you to pay for me."

"It doesn't matter," I say. "It's either that or you'll continue living in fear of being found out, or you leave. We don't have much of a choice here, Vera. We don't. I wish we did. I wish this was easier."

She chews on her lip for a few beats, then stares at the ground. "Common law. We're common law, we've been living together for at least six months. Can we do something through that? In Canada it's a legally binding thing."

"I doubt in Canada that people can get extended visas or permits due to shacking up with someone. Otherwise, there wouldn't be much tragedy in overseas romances, would there?"

"Tragedy?" she asks.

"Let's just say the path we chose, out of all paths, isn't the easiest one."

"No shit, Sherlock."

I glance at her. "Sherlock Holmes?"

She give me a wry but tired smile. "Another expression."

"Of course." I clasp my hands together and close my eyes.

After a thick moment she says, "Please don't think I don't appreciate it."

I only grunt in response.

"It's just a lot of money. A lot of money. Fifteen thousand euros for one year. I could never carry that kind of guilt on me."

"You carry too much guilt on you as it is," I tell her, eyes still closed.

"Nothing more than I deserve."

My eyes fly open and I look at her sharply. "Vera. Stop it. You don't deserve anything but happiness. Get it out of your silly head that this is something you're owed. It's not. You never did anything wrong. You were never the one who was married."

She swallows and looks away. "I am a home-wrecker," she says quietly. "I'm the bad guy."

"No," I say, my voice hard. I spear my words. "*I* am the bad guy. That will never change. But you, you are anything but. You are pure and wonderful and warm and sweet and—"

"A whore."

"Vera," I say, anger and frustration rising through me at lightning speed. I grab her hand. "Don't you dare ever call yourself that. You are not a homewrecker. You are not a whore. You don't deserve to get fired. You don't deserve to leave. You don't even deserve me, but I'm here now, and I'm going to try my hardest to get us out of this. We can be okay if only you'd just let me. Please, Estrella, let me try. This is as much for me as it is for you." I lift her hand to my lips and kiss her knuckles. "I can't lose you. I won't."

She peers at me intensely, perhaps trying to match my own expression, perhaps searching for the truth. "You won't."

"Then let me try."

She nods slowly. "Okay."

I break into a grin. Suddenly nothing seems impossible. "Monday then, you go into Las Palabras, and you leave making them regret this. Take your lipsticks, all your stuff. Never look back. Hold your head up high like the star that you are. Then we'll start taking a look at the school stuff, exactly what we need."

She fidgets. "And you're sure that this will be okay, me staying here illegally?"

"Vera. They will have to step over my dead body to take you away," I say. "Besides, I've always wanted to harbor an alien. Though, when I was young, of course it was an actual alien. You know, like E.T., yes?"

"That's so dated," she says.

I cock my head thoughtfully. "Well, I am an old man."

Her face falls and she quickly averts her eyes. "I'm really sorry about that."

"I know."

She slides her cool fingertips across the stubble on my cheeks, on my jaw, like she's feeling me for the first time. "You are not old. You are perfect. More than that, you are perfect for me. I couldn't, wouldn't, want you any other way than just the way you are now."

"An old man?"

She raises her brow in impatience. "A *beautiful* man."

I think I can live with that.

Chapter Six

The next Wednesday afternoon, I end up working late because Warren had to fly back to the UK for a family emergency. It wouldn't normally be a big deal except that Wednesday is the day I have Chloe Ann, and while Pedro has permitted me to leave early so far—I am just an observer after all—today he does not. I'm tempted to call Isabel and tell her I can't make it, but I am caught up in the idea that Isabel may use that against me. She may think of me as unreliable and not a good father, even though I try everything in my power to be the opposite of that.

Still, it's something I consider until Vera tells me not to worry about it, that she'll handle it. Chloe Ann has a sort of summer day camp on Wednesday mornings so that Isabel can have the entire day off and Vera has come with me to this camp to pick her up at noon on numerous occasions. She's even driven there once or twice, so I have no worries about her wielding the SUV through Madrid's bottleneck traffic and volatile drivers.

When I finally get home though, around six in the evening, I find a different scene at the apartment than the one I had expected.

Chloe Ann is sitting in front of the TV, staring up at it with big, glazed eyes. Vera is on the balcony drinking a beer.

I have to admit, my first thought isn't a good one. Vera is not supposed to be a babysitter, someone to plunk my child in front of the television so she can go drink. She and Chloe Ann are supposed to spend quality time together. It is important to me, more important than it is to either of them.

"Hi, darling," I say to Chloe Ann as I crouch down beside her. My eyes flit to the window where I see Vera noticing me. I kiss my daughter on her head. "How are you?"

She gives me a sweet smile and then looks back to the television where some obnoxious cartoon is playing. They don't make them like they used to.

"Fine, Papa," she says.

I nod and sit down on the ground beside her. "Just fine?" I ask, resting my arms on my knees and looking between her and the TV. "Why is Vera outside?"

"I don't know," she says with a little shrug.

"How was camp today?" I ask.

"Fine, Papa," she says, and for a moment I think the television has stolen her soul, but then she looks to me and smiles more genuinely. "We got to make pretend a petting zoo."

"I bet you were a panda."

"I tried," she says with a pout. "But they said it wasn't allowed at this zoo. I was a goat. It was fun."

"That's great, darling," I tell her, and get to my feet. I stare at her for a few moments, at the light brown hair spilling down her back, the once-neat braids that Isabel had made for her this morning now all messy and rough, then I make my way over to the balcony.

"Is everything okay?" I ask Vera as I step through the sliding door.

She's not looking at me; her attention is on the apartment across the street, but she swallows, jaw tense. "It's okay."

"As long as it's not *fine*," I say, taking the seat across from her. "Then you would sound just like Chloe Ann."

Vera brings her eyes over to mine, and they are full of worry. She looks exhausted too, her face sallow.

"What happened?" I ask, my eyes darting into the living room, making sure Chloe Ann is still there.

"A lot of things," she says, and her voice is hoarse. "I had a bad day."

"Chloe Ann is all right?"

She nods. "Yeah. She's all right. We've been . . . fighting, I guess."

I raise my brows. "Fighting?"

"Not physically."

"Well, no, but what are you talking about?"

She exhales heavily and her shoulders slump forward. "It all started when I picked her up. I was standing around with the others. You know, the other parents. I came early, so I was waiting for it to be over. The kids were all in a circle talking, and we were all just standing around. Everyone knew each other. But one girl came up to me and started speaking in Spanish. And I didn't really understand. I mean, I got the gist of it, but I told her that I didn't speak Spanish very well, that I was learning. She asked why I was there. She spoke English after all. I told her I was there to pick up Chloe Ann." She takes a deep breath, and for some reason my heart already hurts, that I know where this story is going.

"And the girl says, oh, interesting, and I know she's trying to figure out why a non-Spanish speaker like myself has my child at this camp, so I say she's not my child. And even then it was fine because the girl nods, understanding and stuff. But then this fucking bitch who was like fucking listening to the whole thing comes over in her Balenciaga bag and her Louboutin shoes, and her overtanned yoga body and starts speaking rapid-fire Spanish to the girl, who then looks at me like I'm fucking white trash."

"I'm sorry," I find myself saying, but Vera plows on.

"And I guess that would be fine, I mean I can only imagine what this woman is saying, but at least I can play dumb and save face. So I'm standing there with this frozen smile on my face, and then the kids are dismissed, and Chloe Ann comes over just as the woman is still spewing her vile bullshit. I thought maybe it would go over her head, but it didn't because then later we were in the car, and Chloe Ann, she turns to me and says something like, 'why are you pretending to be my mother' or 'you're not my mother,' and . . ." A tear escapes Vera's eye and I reach over to brush it away, but she puts her hand up to keep me back. "And I tried to tell Chloe that I wasn't her mother, but I was her friend and her father's friend. But my Spanish, I'm not sure she understood. And then she started crying, saying she wanted her dad and her mom, and that she *hated* me."

"Oh, Vera. Estrella," I say to her.

"But that's not all."

"That's not? How can there be more?"

"I felt so bad about everything, that on the way home I stopped at an ice cream shop and told Chloe Ann she could have whatever she wanted. It didn't stop her crying, but she still came with me in the shop and I got her mint chocolate chip, and then . . ." She pauses to wipe her eyes. "Then as we were leaving, this fucker appeared and started taking pictures of us. Chloe Ann started crying more, and I fingered the guy, just fucking screaming at the guy to leave."

"Good," I tell her, putting my hand on her bare knee and squeezing it. "I'm glad you did that."

"Yeah, but now that will be in the papers."

I shrug, pretending it doesn't mean what it could. I don't want to add to Vera's guilt complex. "Maybe, maybe not. But does this mean that they were following you?"

"I don't know," she says feebly. "It was your car, maybe they know what to look for."

"The photographer never said anything to you?"

She shakes her head. "No, he just took the picture. When I started yelling, he did fuck off like I asked him to. But still, I think Chloe Ann was traumatized."

"She's fine, Vera. She's inside watching a cartoon. She told me she got to be a goat at camp today. That's all that is sticking out in her head."

"She hates me," she spits out in defeat.

"No, no, no," I say, grabbing Vera's beautiful face in my hands. "She does not hate you. She is my daughter, and you are my lover, and there is only love between you two. She is just young, that is all. She is fine. It's the women at the day camp I have to worry about. I'll talk to them, don't worry about that."

She squeezes her eyes shut. "Mateo, please," she says painfully. "Don't try to fix another problem. Just let them be. Let those bitches say what they want."

"There is a difference between saying what they want and saying it in front of my daughter. I won't let Chloe Ann be fed lies about you and me. That isn't fair to her or to us, or even to Isabel." I let go of her and stand up. "Now come inside and we'll order in dinner tonight. You can tell Chloe Ann she can order whatever she likes."

Vera looks unsure, but I grab her arms and haul her up to her feet. "Stop hiding out here and go inside. Chloe Ann is fine, you'll see."

For a moment I think Vera is going to set up camp outside forever, but then she brushes back her hair, squares her shoulders, and marches past me into the apartment. The fact that she's acting like that, trying to impress my young daughter, does curious things to my heart. I can't help thinking, for all her youth and insecurity, Vera would make a wonderfully caring and compassionate mother one day.

And as Chloe Ann warms to Vera again, and we all settle in for a night of pizza and cartoons, the thought builds and builds and builds until it's all that I can think about.

For now, though, there are other things to get through first.

Over Thursday and Friday, Vera and I are vigilant about looking for the latest news from the gossip magazines. Though we don't say it, I know she is as convinced as I am that the photo of her and Chloe Ann is going to turn up somewhere.

When it appears on Friday afternoon, on a magazine's website, I am almost relieved. The search is over. There it is, the bloody untruth of it all.

Fortunately, I find it when I am at home with Vera and not at my office. Pedro could have lost his mind over that because what the magazine says, it's not good for Atlético's image, and especially not for mine.

It's just one picture, but that picture tells a thousand half-truths: Chloe Ann is in tears and trying to get away from Vera who is holding on to her hand tightly, her other hand extended into the middle finger which hasn't been blurred out. Vera's face is angry, brows pinched, lips in a sneer. For a moment I am grateful that she's not in her pin-up dresses as usual but in capri pants and a conservative tank top, otherwise the press would have something terrible to say about that. She knew how to look when she went to pick her up.

The article talks about how unhappy my daughter is with Vera—the homewrecking Canadian girl—and how divorce affects so much more than just the parent. Like usual, there are a lot of exclamation points and hyperbole and bold statements that accompany most of the garbage out there in these magazines.

As I sit there looking at that on the Macbook, Vera appalled and reading over my shoulder, I feel so much rage that I feel I might die in it. I look at the name of the man who wrote the article—Carlos Cruz, who is also the photographer, I'm guessing the one with the mullet—and I'm immediately planning out how I can hunt him down and beat him to within an inch of his life.

Once again, Vera apologizes, and once again I have to convince her that it isn't her fault. She did the right thing—the sweetest thing—and the paparazzi got her at a bad time, which is always the best time for them. I tell her that this will blow over, that it's not saying anything we haven't seen before.

I believe it all too, I really do.

And then I get a phone call.

From Isabel.

I stare at the screen of the phone as it sits in my hand, and I know, I know, why she's calling. She's seen this exact same thing. Either she was looking for it, found it on her own, or someone tipped her off about it, but she's seen it. I place the computer on Vera's lap and get up. My hand, as I put the phone to my ear, is shaking slightly.

"Hello?" I answer.

I hear air being sucked in through teeth.

"Mateo," Isabel says, her tone carved out of ice and snow. "We need to talk."

I clear my throat. "We are talking."

"No," she says, and it's then that I realize how badly she's restraining herself. There is a warble in her voice underneath all the steel. She's about to lose it. "You come here. And then we'll talk."

I glance at Vera who is staring at me, stricken, like she knows. I wonder if there is any use in pretending that I have no idea what Isabel wants to talk about, but I decide there is no point. It's all going to come out anyway.

"All right," I say. "When? Monday?"

"Right. Now."

I am a dead man. Isabel has to be beside herself if she's seen the article. No one wants to admit they are afraid of their ex-wife, but I am.

"Okay," I say. "I'll leave now."

"Leave the tramp at home," she commands, and then hangs up before I can say anything.

I swallow and stare down at the phone for a beat before I shoot Vera a wary smile. "Isabel. I think she knows. I have to go."

Vera looks like she wants to protest, but she only nods, her knuckles strained as she absently grips the computer. "Okay," she says in a small voice. "I'm sorry."

"Vera, stop," I say, raising my hand. "I don't want to hear any more apologies out of you." I sigh. "Why don't you look online for a restaurant we haven't tried before? When I get back, we'll go out to eat, get drunk, have sex. Sounds good, yes?"

Food, alcohol, and sex are three of her most favorite things, but the suggestion doesn't even bring a smile to her face, just a wan shrug of her shoulders. She is really hurting. I want to stay and comfort her, but that will have to come later, and at that point I have a feeling she may be the one comforting me.

The drive to Isabel and Chloe Ann's takes far longer than it should have. Friday evening traffic seems to be extra mad today, and I actually see two people in a fist fight at the side of their gridlocked cars. The heat is getting to everyone, and even though the air conditioner in the SUV is on full blast, I imagine what would happen if it suddenly conked out. I, too, would probably jump out of the car and start taking on the world, standing on the roof and beating my fists against my chest.

This month has been madness.

When I finally reach the house—my old house—I feel like a poorly wound watch. I take in a deep breath and head up to the front door. The small slice of front yard is as immaculate as always—you would never guess that a small child lives here. That is all Isabel, of course.

I ring the doorbell instead of knocking. It feels weird to even do both when I used to waltz right in. This was my home for seven years. Now it is a stranger's house.

When Isabel answers the door, she is a picture of simmering fury. Though her short blonde blob is slicked in a severe side part and she's wearing a simple dress that shows off years of yoga and pilates, her shoulders are stiff, her face is red, and her eyes are as sharp as razors, ready to draw blood. I'm sure when she opens her mouth her tongue will be the same.

"Isabel," I say cordially, though I'm not smiling either.

"You're late," she seethes.

I look at my watch and shrug. "Traffic. I wasn't aware I was being timed."

Her eyes narrow. "I have a hard time believing that you're not aware of something."

And so we are already headed into sentences with double meanings. Time to face this head on.

"Why did you call me over here, Isabel?"

I step into the foyer that still smells like lemons and wood polish, and she slams the door behind me. "You know very well why you're here."

And then she erupts into a flurry of the most interesting graphic insults and swear words that I have ever heard, each one of them fired at me like a weapon. As usual, they bounce off my skin. I am almost impressed by the names she calls me, tossing around blanket statements like "bad father" and "mid-life crisis," and "endangering our daughter," but it isn't until she pulls Vera's name into this that I've had enough.

"It wasn't like she asked for it," I throw back at her, trying to control my temper. "She was just taking Chloe Ann to get ice cream."

"My daughter is lactose intolerant!" she yells, horrified.

I frown. "What? No she isn't."

"Yes she is! And do you know how much sugar is in ice cream? I will not have a fat daughter who gets diabetes before she's in high school."

I raise my brows to the heavens. "Isabel, seriously. She's a child, children eat ice cream, and she's not and never has been lactose intolerant. You feed her cheese all the time. Are you more upset about that or the picture?"

She takes a step toward me, her nails out, and I'm not sure if she's going to go for her usual slap or not. I stand my ground and don't look away. "You have been making me look like a fool all over again. You know, everyone was talking about Vera the other week, her dancing with that kid in the club, and I was happy. Really, I was happy because she was making you look like the fool for once. But then there were more pictures, the two of you, out for dinner, out for a walk, and then of my daughter with that wretched little tramp, and every time the magazines talk about our divorce, every time they remind me that you threw me aside just to get some young lips around your dick from some fat foreign slut, and—"

"Shut the fuck up!" I yell at her, taking a hard step so I'm right in her face, bearing over her. "You shut your fucking face and keep your vile words to yourself, or this is going to get really ugly."

She doesn't back down. "It's already ugly!" She throws her hands up to the ceiling. "You got my daughter featured in that swill!"

"She's my daughter too!" I roar back. "Don't you think it bothers me?"

She gives me a contemptuous look. "I think you thank god every time I'm made to look like an idiot. I think you've been thanking him a lot lately."

I turn away, burying my face in my hands, and let out a desperate moan. "Isabel, please. Just listen to me. None of this was done on purpose, it was just unfortunate. You know that being back with Atlético will push some attention my way again, but it will all blow over."

"All this time," she says softly. The change in tone is jarring, and I have to look at her. "All this time you could have done something with yourself and you didn't. Not until you left me. Not until now."

I frown, puzzled. "Uh, Isabel. I owned a restaurant until recently, an extremely successful one that you pushed me towards. I am fairly sure that counts as doing something with myself."

She looks at me pointedly. "You know exactly what I mean."

And I do. But how am I supposed to explain that meeting Vera made me realize I was living the wrong life? It would mean nothing to Isabel, and it would only add fuel to the fire.

"Where is Chloe Ann?" I ask, changing the subject.

"Upstairs."

"What? You called me over here for a fight when she's upstairs!?" My throat tightens, and I crane my neck to see up the staircase. Luckily Chloe Ann isn't there. "How dare you let her be exposed to this? Don't you think she's gone through enough already?"

She shrugs and taps manicured nails against her thin lips. "Well, I'm sure she's used to it by now. This is nothing compared to being made a fool of to the entire nation. My god, Mateo. What kind of girl are you seeing, huh? Making my little girl cry like that."

My hands curl and uncurl. "Little girls cry all the time. It wasn't anything Vera did."

"Except stealing her father away from her. That's what she did."

"You don't get it."

"No. I don't. And I'm glad. If I were to understand you and your motivations, that would mean I have
the brains of a snake."

"Are you sure that you don't?"

"You watch yourself, Mateo. I mean it." The way
she focuses on me, just like the reptile she says she's not,
I know she's being serious. "Don't make me change
things for you, because I will."

"Are you threatening me?"

She looks down at her pointy shoes. "No. I'm
not. And I know I'd have to build a really good case
against you if I wanted to take Chloe Ann away from you.
You won your rights fair and square, didn't you?" She
looks up, and we know she's talking about the money I
paid her off with. "But if I see anything like this again, I
can't promise that other people won't take some kind of
action."

"Action? What the hell are you talking about?
Other people?"

She lifts one brow and a malicious little smile tugs
at her lips. I know what she means, at least the people
part. Her family. The blue bloods who once had ties to
the royal Spanish bloodline, the most pretentious, bitter
in-laws you could have. "Just keep my daughter out of the

papers. And keep yourself out of it, too. If me or my family have to be dragged through the mud one more time, things won't be so easy anymore. You know that you got off easy with all of this, don't you?"

I wiggle my jaw back and forth to relieve the tension, but I don't say anything. I just push past Isabel and leave. But when I'm out at the car and I hear the door slam shut, I can't help but turn around. Chloe Ann is at the second story window, hugging her plush panda bear close to her, staring at me with big eyes.

My heart shatters into pieces. I raise my hand to wave at her but she only turns and moves away from the window, disappearing into the darkness of the room. It takes all that I have not to break down, not to lose it. I get in the car and take a few moments to regain my composure, to slow my heart, to will away the dull ache inside. Isabel was right. I did get off easy. Everything before seems easy compared to the pain of right now and the pain that I know will follow.

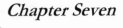

Chapter Seven

I'm starting to feel like a prisoner in my own house. I don't mind it so much, but Vera seems restless, like a caged animal. When I get back from Isabel's, we decide not to chance having our photographs taken again and just stay inside for the evening. We order greasy Chinese food and finish off two bottles of expensive wine from my makeshift cellar in the front closet, but I know Vera is itching to go outside and let loose. She's a bit drunk, as I am, and though we are feeling unfettered, I know the feeling is temporary. It's a Band-Aid, but it's a warranted one. We need to ignore the wounds for now.

It's late when the phone rings, and once again it's Isabel. I sigh, giving Vera a tired look, and she nods, heading toward the washroom with her glass of wine. She doesn't need to give me privacy, but it makes me feel better if she's not within earshot of my ex-wife's potentially vile words.

Thankfully, Isabel is brief. She tells me that she's taking Chloe Ann to see her parents over the weekend and I won't be able to see her. I would normally take issue with this, but I let it pass. It worries me, as it should, that this could be the start of a new pattern, but at the moment I don't really feel I have a leg to stand on. The wine wouldn't help me win any argument either.

"Hell hath no fury like a woman scorned."

I turn in my chair as I put the phone back into my pocket and give Vera a curious look as she walks toward me. Yet another English saying that I don't know. "I'm afraid I don't understand."

She gives me a soft but tired smile and sits down on the armrest. I immediately wrap my arm around her waist and pull her down into my lap, where she comes to a rest with a tipsy giggle, her hair obscuring the impish smile on her face.

"Explain," I demand. "Or I will punish you with kisses."

She raises her brow. "Followed by punishment with penis?"

I shrug, glad she's acting playful. "That can be arranged. Now tell me, my Estrella."

She sighs and buries her lips into my neck. I can't help the small moan that escapes from me, nor my hardness building beneath her ass. It would feel so good—*so good*—to just succumb to the physical, to take all this mental anguish away. I close my eyes and fight the urge to pick her up and take her to the bedroom, the only other way I know how to make her feel safe and sated, the only way I know how to escape during a time like this.

"Hell hath no fury like a woman scorned," she says against my throat, "is a saying. I don't know where it's from but it means nothing is scarier than a pissed off bitch." She pauses, sucking in her breath, and I know she fears she's said the wrong thing. "Sorry," she quickly adds, and I feel her body tense up beneath my fingers. "I didn't mean that Isabel is a bitch."

She is still so skittish over her words these days, it's like she's second guessing every aspect of her being. I cup the back of her head with my hand and let the softness of her hair wash over me. "I know you didn't," I assure her. "And, well, she is being a bitch." And that's a major understatement.

"Can you blame her though?" she asks, her voice rising in pitch, and when she pulls away from me, her eyes are wet. It breaks my heart. I'm getting tired of my heart breaking, and I know that this isn't going to change anytime soon. Every day there is another weight on us and another crack appears.

"No," I tell her honestly. "I cannot blame her."

A silence lapses over us, heavy like a cloak.

Finally she clears her throat. "She's going to hurt for a long time," she says. "She's going to be angry. This isn't going away. I thought everything was behind us now, that she'd move on. You've been divorced for a year, if she's still this mad a year out . . ."

"She is mad because I am back with Atlético," I tell her. "She is mad because of the paparazzi, the way they are hounding us again. She is mad because she feels she is being made to look like a fool. If I had just stayed with my head down, she wouldn't be doing this."

"But you can't live your life in fear, Mateo," she tells me.

I smile at her and brush her sunset hair from her face. "And neither can you."

She settles back against my body—sinks, conforms, melds. She is a second skin. She is a part of myself

I can't bear to separate from. I pray I never have to. I pray we can survive whatever is coming our way.

And I can feel it coming, that tension, that storm rolling in with each day. I'm so terribly afraid that my plan isn't going to work, that she will be found out, that she won't find a job, that she won't get into the school. I'm so afraid the stars will take their brightest one away from me.

I pick her up in my arms, and for all her pillowy curves, she weighs nothing more than a feather. I take her down the hall to the bedroom and throw her on the bed. She glows in the ochre lights from the street that stream in through our windows, and it isn't long before we are both naked and I am climbing over her, pinning her arms above her head and drinking in her body like the most beautiful, decadent wine.

I will devour her until all of this is gone.

I will consume her until we are all that's left.

I push inside her and let my hunger take over.

I let my hunger take us to a better place. Hot, slow, and fleeting.

Fleeting.

When we wake up the next morning, tangled in each other's arms, the sun shining through the windows, it feels like we only have each other and that's all that is left.

Maybe it has always been that way.

I throw myself into my work. I get to the stadium early, and I leave late but it doesn't do anything to discourage the photographers who are sometimes waiting by the road just for a glimpse of me. I can't understand it, why even a photo of me getting into a car means something to them, and after a while I stop trying.

Vera keeps busy too, filling out all the paperwork for school and laying low. Several times Claudia has called or come by, and while they have fun drinking and dancing around the living room, I'm starting to feel like a parent who has grounded a kid. She even forgoes her Spanish class, and I teach her instead. As much as I don't like it when Vera goes out, I realize that she needs to let loose and have fun. She's too free of a spirit to be cooped up, even when there's plenty of sex to distract her.

When Wednesday morning rolls around, I pick up Chloe Ann from her day camp. Vera stays at home—this time with no objection—and I head over there with a plan in mind. I wasn't kidding when I said I wanted to talk to these mothers at the camp to set them straight.

When I walk into the school building where the camp is held, I'm immediately met with hostile eyes. Every single woman is staring right at me with the same expression: pursed lips, a single raised brow, a discerning glance.

Chloe Ann runs right to me.

"Papa!" she cries out, throwing her arms around my leg. "You came."

"Lucky thing," one woman with terribly dark lip liner whispers to another. "She doesn't have to be traumatized by that *puta* again."

I eye the woman sharply. "Excuse me?" I say loud enough for everyone to hear.

The woman doesn't look afraid. She pastes on a fake smile that looks like a chalk outline. "How are you, Mateo? We missed you last week. At least, your daughter seemed to."

"Papa," Chloe Ann cries out, pulling on my trousers. "Can we go, please?"

I place a kind hand on the top of her head. "Just a minute, darling," I tell her, then turn my attention back to the woman. "You know, I and I'm sure any parent here, would appreciate if you didn't use such words in front of the children."

The daycare teacher, Mrs. Caro, looks up from putting toys away in a box. She's the only woman who looks concerned. All the other women are still staring at me with utter hatred in their eyes. It's only now that I realize the look has always been there, I've just never noticed. Of course they hate the man that screwed over one of their own, and of course they hate Vera, whom they consider the whore—the other woman.

"I don't know what you're talking about," the lip liner woman says haughtily. "If anyone is saying bad words around your daughter, it's not me. Perhaps you should go ask your teenage girlfriend what she's been saying. Maybe she needs her mouth washed out with soap."

The woman elapses into a fit of giggles, leaning against her friend while all the children are oblivious. She's oblivious too, to that fact that out of everyone, she's the one who is acting like a teenager.

I can't stoop to her level. I won't give her a reaction.

I stand tall and grab Chloe Ann's hand and lead her away. The woman calls out behind me, "Give my regards to Isabel. Tell her we miss her."

I suck in my breath but keep going. We are in the parking lot, almost at the car, when the mullet-headed photographer appears out of nowhere and starts taking pictures, the bulbs flashing.

I immediately step in front of Chloe Ann, shielding her from the lights, from the lens, and I can hear her whimper in fright behind me.

"Get out of my face," I sneer at the photographer, putting my arm out in front of me. I want nothing more than to let loose a string of expletives, but considering what I had just said earlier, it would make me hypocritical.

Still, this situation calls for it more than anything else.

"Is your daughter being abused, Mr. Casalles?"

The question catches me so off-guard that my mouth drops open, and I can only blink until a flashbulb blinds me again.

"I beg your fucking pardon?" So much for not swearing.

"Your daughter," the man continues. Click, click, *click*. "She was crying, distressed when I last saw her. Your girlfriend, is she abusing her?"

"What the fuck?" I yell, fist raised, and Chloe Ann cries. I quickly grab her, unlock the car, place her inside, and shut the door, the tinted windows protecting her from the scene.

I whirl around to face him like I'm facing an attacker. "Now, please, what the fuck are you talking about? No one is abusing anyone. My girlfriend picked up my daughter from day camp. They had ice cream. My daughter was upset about something or other as little girls do, and you, asshole, decided that was a great fucking time to take the damn picture. If anyone is abusing anyone around here, it's you. Stalking me every fucking place I go, terrorizing me, my girlfriend, my daughter. You're disgusting." I turn around to put my hand on the door handle. "And if I see your face again, I'm going to rip your head right off."

The photographer stops shooting for a moment, and the pause is enough that I turn around to look at him. He's staring at me with a strange smile on his face. "Are you threatening me, Mr. Casalles?" he asks. "I think you might be. *Mr. Casalles threatens local journalist as he stands on the brink of another mid-life crisis.* Why don't you make things easier for me and tell me what pussy you're going to trade your current model in for?"

139

I don't think. I barely feel. I just throw the punch.

I manage to bypass the camera and hit him square in the nose. I was always good at getting it in the goal. He yelps in pain, and his camera goes smashing to the ground. I don't think anything has ever felt so satisfying, but the feeling only lasts a moment until I hear Chloe Ann crying from the car.

I've really screwed up this time. I can hear voices behind me, and some of the mothers from the day camp have seen the whole thing. I hope they got everything that led up to the hit too, but knowing their single-minded vindictiveness, it probably wouldn't make a difference.

And so, I panic. As the photographer, holding his nose and swearing his head off, stoops down to gather up his shattered camera, I get in the car and quickly start the engine. I peel backward out of the parking lot—Chloe Ann sniffling in the backseat—and onto the road.

I leave the incident behind, but I know it won't leave me.

When I get home, Vera has left a note that she has gone out for a short walk. Chloe Ann has calmed down, and I try to explain to her why daddy did what he did. It's difficult because what I want to instill in my daughter is the ability to shoulder what life throws at her without getting physical or losing composure. I don't want her to believe that it's okay to hurt someone just because they hurt you.

I think I've gotten through to her; she seems to understand, nodding her small head and staring down at her little hands.

When Vera comes back, she immediately sees something is wrong. Thankfully, Chloe Ann is smiling now and doesn't seem to harbor any resentment toward her.

"I messed up," I tell Vera, and I realize how stricken my voice sounds.

Her face crumples and she grabs my hand, leading me over to the couch.

"Tell me," she implores, sitting down and pulling me down beside her.

Knowing that Chloe Ann is preoccupied with a coloring book and can't understand English at any rate, I launch into it from the start, from arriving at the day camp and having to deal with those horrible women, to driving away from the scene of the crime, Chloe Anne crying in the back.

I place my face in my hands, lean over my knees, and try and hide myself from the world. Vera rubs her hand slowly up and down my back but doesn't say anything. There is no "it's going to be okay" because how on earth is everything going to be okay? How could it? Things were bad before, and I just drove that last nail in. It doesn't matter that I may have had the right to lash out, but I know this photographer and the parasite that he is, and he won't take this lying down.

"He's going to press charges," I mumble into my hands.

Her rubbing pauses. "He said that?"

"I just know."

And I'm right. The next morning I receive a phone call from the police department informing me to get a lawyer because Mr. Carlos Cruz wants to charge me for assault. I end up taking a sick day from work just to get everything all sorted—the last thing I want is for Pedro to know about this, and I need to do all that I can in order to keep it under the covers.

I knew it won't be easy. My lawyer, whom I had seen far too much of over the past year, tells me there is a good chance this won't go to court and that it can be settled otherwise with large sums of dough. Apparently I am good at paying people off. But he isn't too optimistic about it staying out of the papers, not in the meantime anyway.

When I drop off Chloe Ann at her mother's house, I am tempted to just tell her everything right there. That way it won't be a surprise when she reads about it. But somehow I can't bring myself to do it. There is this tiny little hope inside me, shining dimly, that perhaps Mr. Cruz will be so ashamed or embarrassed about the incident that it won't make the tabloids at all.

It is only later that I realize I should have said something. Even if the photographer doesn't speak, there is a chance Chloe Ann might if Isabel asks her about her stay. To say I spent the rest of Thursday a nervous wreck is an understatement.

Now it's Friday. It's ten a.m. and I'm back at my desk, absently watching old plays and winning goals on my computer in an attempt to better understand the team. I can barely concentrate. I am pretty much useless. My knuckles hurt, but I bet his face hurts even more.

There is a knock at my door. I turn around in my seat to see Pedro on the other side of the glass, motioning for me to open it. I don't know why he doesn't just come in since it's not locked, but he is the type of guy to engage in minor power struggles throughout the day.

I slowly ease myself out of the chair and stride over to the door. "Yes, sir?" I ask as I open it, eyeing him inquisitively. He looks the same as ever—a slack smile with hardened eyes—so I can't read what this is about.

"Mateo." He says my name like he's not sure if it's mine. "How are you feeling?"

"Much better," I tell him. "Stomach bug."

There is an almost imperceptible raise of his brow. "Good. Glad to hear you're better. Listen . . . can I come in?"

I try not to swallow the brick in my throat. "Of course," I tell him, stepping aside.

He folds his arms and looks around the office. "Where is Warren?"

"With Diego," I tell him. "Downstairs."

"Good," he says again. "Mateo," he says, and then pauses as if he's holding his breath. I wait for the worst. He already knows. I'm fired.

"I think we might move you into Warren's position first before you take over Diego's. We'll be looking to do this in October. Is that okay with you?"

I blink a few times. "I'm sorry?"

His grey brows furrow together as if I should know this already. "We think you're ready. I do, anyway. It's better to get rid of Warren now."

"Uh, but sir, I thought Warren would stay assistant coach to me?"

He smiles cautiously. "Ah, Mateo. Such naïve thoughts. Warren knows now that he's not going anywhere. You took the ceiling from him. He's better off with another team. He'll have no problem finding one, preferably in England."

It seems like all the English speakers are getting fired these days. I don't know what to say, only that I personally don't think I'm ready to be Atlético's assistant coach. We haven't even had our first official game of the season yet—that starts next week.

"Why are you waiting until October when the league is in full swing?"

He shrugs. "Gives you some time to see the team in real action."

"And who are you hiring for his position?"

Another shrug and he turns for the door. "We shall see." From the tone of his voice, it sounds like it's just shooting fish in a barrel for him.

He leaves, shutting the door behind him, and all at once I feel like the walls are caving in on me. I should be elated about moving into Warren's role so soon, but it's hard to feel anything but overwhelmed, especially when I can't seem to get a handle on anything and my personal life is on the verge of exploding into something I may not recover from.

And I go from the verge to the middle of a full-blown fire. At three p.m., after Diego and Warren and Pedro have all left early, as they usually do on Fridays, I get a text from Vera.

Have you seen it?

I haven't, and I don't need to ask what she's talking about.

I take in a deep breath and try to steady my shaking hands as I click on the bookmarked page for the Diez Minutos site.

Vera texts me again, but I can't look at the phone. My eyes are glued to the screen. It's about as bad as I feared. Maybe more, maybe less, and somehow knowing that this was going to happen doesn't make it seem like less of a surprise.

It's front page of the site this time, and maybe that's why it causes the actual hairs on the back of my neck to stand up, for my chest to fill with concrete and quicksand.

Future Atlético Coach and Ex-Football Star Attacks Photographer.

There are three pictures. One is of me walking with Chloe, trying to shield her from his lens. The other is of me yelling at him, spittle flying out of my lips. The last is one of Carlos—the after shot—with his purple bruised eye and nose. He doesn't look horrible, but he's definitely adding to it with his pained expression.

The article does not paint the truth. It paints a lie. It says that I saw him and went irate, wanting revenge for past wrongdoings. I apparently hit him completely unprovoked, smashed his camera, and then sped off from the scene of the crime. That last part is true, of course, but the amount of pure bullshit in his words is unbelievable.

To make matters worse, he actually interviewed the woman with the lip liner, that immature *puta*. It turns out her name is Maria Francisco, the wife of a local politician for some lesser-known party. She says that she knew I was "bad news" when I came to pick up Chloe Ann, and was already antagonizing her and other ladies at the day camp for no apparent reason. She notes that she wasn't surprised this happened at all, and had only wished she could have done something to protect the photographer from my wrath. She had witnessed the punch that I "randomly" threw and then ran over to help. By the time she arrived on the scene, I was gone.

The article goes on to say that the photographer is thinking of pressing charges, and it's only then that I realize he didn't write the article himself. I suppose he figures it is more credible this way.

As I sit back in my chair, the room seems to glow brighter, the fluorescent lights buzzing louder. Everything inside me seems to be caught in a stranglehold. It's like I don't breathe, I don't bleed, I don't have a heartbeat. I feel like my anger is so raw and terrible that it's actually trying to kill me on the spot. I don't think I've ever been this livid, felt so fucking hopeless, in my whole entire life.

I sit like this forever. It feels like forever, seems like forever, and when I finally manage to move, I'm shocked to see that only thirty minutes have passed. I eventually eye my phone and the missed calls and ten panicked texts, all from Vera.

There is nothing to say, really. So I text her that I am on my way home and will see her soon.

When I get into the apartment, I am still in my daze. Vera has been crying, and she's fluttering around like a flightless bird. She's afraid for me, she's afraid for her. She's muttering things about me going off to jail, that she'll be all alone, that she'll never see me again. It doesn't seem to matter that yesterday things seemed more straightened out with the lawyer. Suddenly it's like it hits her, how fragile her life here is, and she seems to lose it right before my eyes.

I do my best to comfort her but it's hard when I don't believe half the shit that's coming out of my mouth. But I have to be strong, even if I don't feel it. I have to be the one to stand tall and get us through this, to hold her above the water, this rising, raging tide.

I'm not sure how it happens—maybe it's the glasses of scotch we down, sitting together in the living room and staring at the bright, hot sunshine outside until it disappears into blue and black, but somehow we get through the day.

Just when I'm about to tell her we should go to bed and see what tomorrow brings, just when I think to myself that we may have gotten off easy, my phone rings.

We both freeze. We know who it is somehow without even looking. I look at Isabel on the call display, and from my stance alone, Vera knows. She places her hand on my shoulder, kisses me softly on the shoulder, and heads to bed.

Isabel is furious. This is nothing new, but her anger has so many levels, it's like the Zelda game I used to play as a kid. Once you unlock them, they just keep coming.

I barely listen. It's everything I thought it would be, and she has no interest in the truth, the fact that this man is a threat to us and our daughter. She just cares about her image, about being made a fool of, how she, by default, looked to those other parents. I think maybe some part of her is happy that I ended up in such a violent act because it's a way for her to show the world that the divorce was a good thing—it gives her some control. But the fact is, her pride speaks louder than anything else, and she's embarrassed she married me in the first place.

When I hang up, I'm not sure where I stand or what's going to happen. I head to bed and curl up beside Vera. Neither of us sleep for the longest time, but when slumber finally does pull me under, it does so with such ferocity that my last hazy thought is the fear I may never wake up.

But when I do the next morning, I'm not sure if it was fear at all but desperate longing.

Chapter Eight

The weekend passes by in a blur. Once again, there is a reason why Chloe Ann can't come see me, and this time I am not afraid to question it. But I am met with resistance from Isabel and excuses. Apparently she had told me a long time ago that she wanted to bring Chloe Ann to a waterpark before the summer was over, and that in this heat it was barbaric to deny her the opportunity to cool down.

I don't like it. In fact, I hate it with every part of me. I feel like this is the beginning of the very slow process of annihilation. But my protests go unnoticed, and I spend the weekend with Vera, trying to get through it with a whirl of heat, haze, and alcohol.

We are afraid to leave the apartment, so we don't. It's prison time again but this time I really do know it's for the better. I just know that Mr. Cruz will be outside, waiting for me, waiting for another attempt, and I know that other reporters will have joined in as well. It's a big story, big enough now that it makes the Sunday edition of El País.

There's my angry face, there's the accusations. You'd think I would be used to this, but I'm not. I had only made Spain's main newspaper years ago when I was back on Atlético. To be featured again, as myself and not a player, is a big deal. It pains me to think that everyone across the country—from my parents to my relatives to my sister, to chumps like Bon and old friends of Isabel's and the people I went to Las Palabras with—they are reading this and shaking their heads, wondering what is happening to me, where I went wrong. I ditch my wife, take on a younger girlfriend, rejoin Atlético, punch a photographer. It's forever one step forwards, two step backwards. Give and take. The equilibrium of the cosmos.

The worst comes around on Monday morning when I realize I have to leave my apartment to go to work, and once I am at work I will have to face the wrath of the reputation-conscious Pedro.

I get down to the parking garage without incident, but once I pull my car out and onto the street, I can see the crowd of reporters gathering. Some of them start running toward me, flashing their cameras, and it takes a lot to maintain composure, to make sure I'm not hitting anyone as I press down on the gas and drive. You would think there are more important things going on in this crazy, upside down world of ours, but apparently not today. Today it's all about picking on those who don't get their chance to share their side of the story.

Easy targets.

When I get to the stadium, I feel the eyes of everyone burning into me. I can't even smile at them, pretend to be this jovial guy who is just misunderstood. I can't even pretend to be me. I look down, my feet on my wingtips, my expression closed-off and neutral. I don't want them to see any part of me.

My office isn't empty. Warren is standing at his desk, pinning something on the wall. He can't be that young anymore, but with his blonde shaved head, wild eyes, and wiry limbs, he could pass for someone in his twenties. When I step in, he pivots toward me, looking both concerned and extremely impressed.

"Way to go," he says, and he says it in such a way that it takes me a moment to realize he is completely genuine.

"What?" I ask in English as I take my seat and swivel my chair around to face him.

"I hate that bloody fuck," he says. "Do you not remember the time that I got in a brawl with Sebastian? Real Madrid? I was in Arsenal? That fucking wanker photographed the whole thing."

"Carlos Cruz?" I ask, now remembering the time that Warren got in a fight with one of the leftfielders for Real Madrid. This was a long time ago, but most of the football fights stuck out in my head, mainly because you always knew what started it or who provoked it.

He nods. "Yeah. He was the one who took the pictures outside of the nightclub. Anyway, I'm just saying, he's a douche and I'm happy you punched his fucking face in. Especially you, Mateo."

"Why especially me?"

"Because I've been waiting for you to go a bit mad, if you don't mind me saying."

I frown at him. "You have?"

He nods enthusiastically. "Old boy, I've been in your shoes. Not quite, but close. I left my ex-wife, too. Not for someone a lot younger, but someone a lot better. My life was a mess for a long time, and so was Sheila's. She's, you know, the new wife. The only wife. We're still together, you know, despite what all those fucks thought."

"I see."

"I'm just saying, I know what it's like. It's tough to wrong someone, and it's tough to be the one wronging them. But I don't regret it for a second. Neither does Sheila. I can't imagine life without her, so it makes all the bloody bullshit we went through worth it. In fact," he pauses to scratch the golden stubble on his chin, "I think we needed to go through all the shit in order to prove to ourselves—and to the world—that we could handle it, that we were meant for each other. Time went on, as it does, and sooner or later people forgot. Once we got married, my ex eventually found someone else and remarried. My family understood it was serious. Took them bloody long enough, but there you have it. It was worth it."

I am feeling decidedly guilty about Warren now. Not that it was my decision to possibly let him go—that was all Pedro—but the chance of him leaving soon is high, and I'm only now really starting to like him.

He gives me a crooked smile that hides his crooked teeth. "If I can give you advice . . . well, it's not really advice because I fucking don't know much. But whatever you and, Vera, is it? Whatever you have, hang on to it. I know you already know that, I can tell just by looking at you, but what I mean is, you're going to be each other's infinity for a long time. The only rowboat in the storm or whatever bloody anthology—sorry, analogy—there is. But it's just going to be you and her because everyone else is going to pretend that they don't understand." He leans in and winks at me. "Here's the kicker. They do understand. But they don't want to. To understand, they fear, is to become. And they would rather someone else take the heat than them. They stay safe. You stay wild. But in the end, you're happy and you're free, because you did what you knew you had to. Just hang on to her and know that even if it's just the two of you for a while, if it's meant to be, the two of you is really all you need."

He pauses before going to sit down at his desk. "As long as the sex is good, anyway. If it's not, then I don't think anything can help you."

I almost assure him that the sex is more than good, but I have the impression that he knows anyway.

I'm impressed by Warren, and his insight leaves me feeling slightly optimistic. Maybe it's okay if the world is boiled down to just Vera and I. As long as we don't let go of one another, as long as we can work together, as long as the rest of the world, one day, promises to catch up.

My optimism leaves me, though, the minute I get a call from Pedro.

He wants to meet me in his office. Immediately.

I get up and am about to leave when Warren wishes me good luck. Funny thing is, he means it, just as he means everything he said before. I'm not sure what Pedro has in mind for me now, but the fact is I took away Warren's potential career, and I might be taking away his current job, and yet the man doesn't seem to hold any grudges. That fact gives me the smallest bit of courage as I make my way through the halls to see my boss.

He's waiting at his Lucite desk, his office all white sterility. There are no cigars this time, only his long stern face to take in like a dry stogie.

There are no what ifs or guesses. We both know why I'm here.

"Mateo," he says, but that's all he says as he gestures to the seat across from him. For a moment I wish he would just fire me on the spot so I don't have to go through the whole long process of it all. But I still sit down and put on my mask, ready for whatever things he's going to say. At the moment I almost laugh because I'm making him out to be worse than my actual father. Now there is someone whose opinion I care about. Not this guy. Not really.

"I guess you've heard," I tell him.

He manages a wry smile though his eyes remain cold as stone. "Who hasn't?"

"I assume you don't want to know the real story," I tell him, crossing a foot over my knee. I pay attention to my shoes. They seem like the safest place. Nice, glossy brown leather. Top dollar. They were a present of sorts when I sold the restaurant. I try and think about how my life as a restaurateur would have handled this scandal. I think it would have done well for business.

"I'm sure I already know the real story," Pedro says simply. "I've been watching the papers carefully. I can't say I'm surprised that this happened. It seems like you can't take a shit without someone there. In some ways I feel sorry for you, Mateo."

"But . . ." I fill in, because there is always one.

"But," he says, "I do expect better from you. Look, I know you can't help it if you go to the gym and someone follows you, or you go out for dinner and they are there, or Vera goes and does whatever she does and she's photographed. I know you can't live a sheltered life, even if it is for just a short while, until their fascination with you is over. But I do expect a level of decorum from you. And though I can't necessarily blame you for hitting this guy, I would have thought you'd have more respect for the team. For Atlético. And for me. Because you knew what would happen if you hit him, didn't you?"

I barely nod. I feel like a kid again in the principal's office. Back then I got in trouble for my hotheadedness too.

"I wasn't thinking," I tell him, and that is the truth. I remember a distinct lack of thought. It was all action and instinct.

"No, you weren't." He sighs, long and hard. "But I have a daughter. I have two. I know what it's like to try and protect them. I do think this photographer is a vile creature, and I don't think that you're in the wrong. But you need to make sure that you settle this out of court. I don't want a trial, I don't want this drawn out. The focus for this season needs to be on the team, not on you. You cannot be more famous than the players, that's just how it goes."

"And that's how I want it," I tell him. "I promise, there are arrangements being made as we speak. I am more than willing to negotiate to keep this from going on unnecessarily. I can only hope that Cruz will take it."

"He's a bloodsucker," he says. "If it's high enough, he'll take it. Even if it's not that high, it has to seem high to him. Make it seem like you're suffering because of the settlement, and he'll take whatever you give him."

Another good bit of advice, and it's not even noon yet on this horrible day. I give Pedro a curious look, wondering how many incidents like this one he's been involved in. His face gives me nothing, but I feel like his words have given me all I need to know.

Vera has her Spanish class tonight, and for the second week in a row, she thinks she is going to miss it. Yet even though I know we are staying out of trouble and keeping us both safe by staying inside, I know it can't go on like this.

I had an idea earlier in the day. On the way home, once I lost the paparazzi car that was trailing me, I stopped by a party supply store on the edges of the city. I picked up a few things, and then I came straight home.

Her class starts at seven, and at six o'clock I am reaching into the closet and pulling out the shopping bag. I bring it out to the kitchen where she is leaning against the bar, sipping on a glass of red wine and flipping through a fashion magazine, looking bored.

I wave the bag at her. "Guess what I have?"

She shuts the magazine and looks up at me with dull eyes. "What?"

I grin at her, knowing more than she does, and empty out some of the contents onto the counter. A blond mullet wig and a long black Cher one spill over in glossy strands.

"Role playing?" she asks, her eyes starting to sparkle more.

"Maybe later," I tell her. "But for now, it's our way to your Spanish class."

She takes a moment to consider it. "Wait, what?"

I toss her the long black one which she catches. "You put on that, I put on this. We walk out of the building and I take you straight to class. No one will know it's us."

She gives me an unimpressed scowl. "Yeah right they won't know."

"They won't," I say, and tip out the rest of the bag. There's an acid wash denim vest and a big black hoodie with the words "Amsterdam High" printed on it. "The beautiful vest is for me, and the classy sweater is for you."

"You're kidding."

"I'll be laughing soon, but I assure you I am not kidding now." I pick up the mullet and the vest. "You don't believe me?"

I take off my shirt, slip on the godawful vest, and pull on the wig. When I turn to face Vera, she's smiling. It's a pitiful one, brought on because I look like such an idiot, but a smile is a smile and hers are worth millions.

"Oh wow," she says. "You look pretty hot."

I nod at the black wig. "Not as hot as you will be, my Estrella."

She sighs dramatically but still puts on the sweat-shirt and plunks the wig on her head. She straightens it, shiny fake pieces falling in her face, and eyes me. "Are you happy now?"

"It's entirely inappropriate but I'm extremely turned on," I tell her as I look her up and down. "You look like a very bad girl, caught by the police for stealing a six-pack of beer and a bag of marijuana from someone's car."

Her expression becomes seductive. "Well, you know there is nothing inappropriate about being turned on. Not when it comes to me, anyway."

She comes over to me and wraps her arms around me and the stiff vest.

"You have class," I tell her, prying her arms off me.

"You can't tell me what to do."

"I can and I did," I say, smacking her on her plump ass. "Now come on."

"Are we seriously going outside in these?"

I nod. "Very serious. Just for a few blocks, until the photographers are out of sight. Although," I say, turning to the mirror in the hall and admiring my ridiculous image, "I am growing awfully fond of this look."

She rolls her eyes and grabs her bag, then slips the hood up over her black hair.

Moments later we head out the front door, big sunglasses on both of our faces. I hunch down a bit, slumping my shoulders forward, masking my normally great posture, and paste a lazy smile on my face. Vera does the same. We don't look a thing like we normally do—angry and defiant—but even then my heart is racing in my throat, and I am certain we will be found out.

At first their eyes and cameras are all on us, but we are saved by another couple coming toward the building. I know them—Italians, Gio and his blond wife Sophia—and they are just classy enough to distract the cameras. We walk away and are forgotten.

Still, we don't shed our disguises until we are only a few blocks from the building where she takes her classes. While she goes in, I wait outside, grabbing a cup of coffee at a nearby café until she is done and comes out to join me.

Something about being outside, in the night where the air has dared to drop a few degrees, makes me feel more alive than I have in weeks. I can feel it coming off of Vera too, this energy that for once isn't formed from chaos and fear. We both have plenty to be afraid of, but as we walk hand in hand down hushed streets, even with our disguises stuffed inside her overflowing bag we feel anonymous and free. It doesn't mean that we don't get a few odd looks here and there—we do. People recognize us. But we keep walking as if it doesn't mean a thing.

Just as Warren had said, we have each other, and that is all we need. Our own little world in our own little solar system in our own little universe. Tonight, we are infinite.

We go to a bar and stay there for hours. We snack on tapas, drink cool sangria, watch people from our dark booth, talk to each other in Spanish. She is improving.

It's almost a shame to go home, but we both know we must. Tonight has been another Band-Aid, but it's one that we desperately needed or else we would tear at the seams. It feels impossibly good to have all the worries placed aside for now, locked in a heavy steel box, to only think about enjoying life and each other.

A few minutes from the apartment we don our disguises again, and just a block away, I grab Vera by the waist and pull her into a narrow, empty alley. I spin her around so that she's pressed up against the stone wall. I kiss her passionately, tucking the synthetic hairs behind her ears. It may not feel like hers, but her soft mouth certainly does.

She reaches for me, one hand tugging at the band of my pants, the other at my neck. In this moment, both of us look like strangers and both of us are free, yet we choose each other.

It's dirty here in this alley, the wall slick with heat, the ground uneven stone, and we are exposed to the world. But our disguises make me feel safe, and I am driven by the desire of being a wanted man, acting scandalous in plain sight of a city in pursuit.

I bury my lips into her neck, biting, kissing, tasting, and she deftly undoes my belt and unzips my fly. I push her higher up the wall, holding her there, her skirt shoved up around her hips. I take her there, fast and hard, bold and brash. I drive myself in deep, feeling every inch of her, and I am so completely enveloped by her hot tight hold that my eyes roll back in my head. I feel like we're giving the proverbial finger to the world, proving in our own way that it can't keep us down, that we can handle whatever comes our way. It's always more than just sex when it comes to us, and this time is no exception.

After we've both come, she slides down to her feet and falls into my arms. I hold her tight, regaining my composure, and it takes me a moment to realize where we are and where we have to go.

"There's nothing like a little bit of role playing," she jokes as she pulls away from me, her wig askew.

I smile, but inwardly I disagree. That wasn't role playing at all.

We straighten ourselves out and head to the apartment. There are only three photographers outside now—the rest must have given up—and I don't see Carlos among them. I avoid eye contact, and it's only just as we are walking in through the door that I see a flashbulb go off and hear someone yell, "Mr. Casalles!"

But it's too late. We are safe inside, and they only have a picture of the back of my head. It means we can't use these disguises again, but for just the one night together, it was worth it.

Chapter Nine

It was weird The photo of us—me as the redneck and Vera as a Goth queen—is shown in a lesser tabloid the next day, but aside from that there isn't much else to report. On Thursday I get a call from my lawyer, and for once it's good news. It seems as if Mr. Cruz is more than willing to settle out of court. It was probably his plan all along, although I make it clear that if this does happen, he has to promise never to take another photograph or write another article about me or my family again. My lawyer seems to think that won't be a dealbreaker, but I don't dare share his optimism. This month has turned me into a hardened man.

"Baby," I hear Vera purr from beside me. I groan and look at the mahogany clock on the bedside table. It's almost eight a.m. Usually Friday mornings start a little slow, but today I was hoping to get into work early so that I could leave just after lunch. Vera and I have week-end plans to visit San Sebastian on the north coast, and I'm hoping I can convince Isabel to let us take Chloe Ann with us. I think the refreshing waves of the Atlantic will be like a tonic to our overwrought souls, something to re-charge us again. Normally we would take advantage of the condo in Barcelona, but we both know what happened the last time we were there.

I swear in Spanish and quickly roll out of bed. Vera is propped up under the sheets looking like the most irresistible seductress. It's a real pity that I can't stay a few moments longer and enjoy her but it's all about little sac-rifices for the greater good.

On my way to the office I try Isabel's phone, hop-ing to ask about Chloe Ann, but I just get her voicemail. I text her instead and then stop by a corner store to pick up a quick coffee and a handful of gossip magazines. I know it looks ridiculous—a businessman buying these shit sto-ries—but it's almost become a daily ritual for me.

I drive to the stadium and get there with a few minutes to spare. I sit in the SUV, sip my coffee, and then quickly peruse them.

What I see in the first magazine I pick up, on the first page, makes my blood ice over.

The headline boldly states: *The Truth About Mateo Casalles.*

It is not written by Carlos Cruz; instead it's by some woman in a smaller magazine called Caliente. There are no new photos to accompany the story, just one of me cheering after scoring a goal for Atlético, one of me and Isabel leaving my old restaurant, and one of me and Vera kissing on the street, probably taken a year ago.

The photos aren't the focus of the article at any rate. The focus is the lies.

The whole article is about someone, an anonymous source who is apparently close to me, who says they have the whole truth about the situation.

And the scary, terrible, disturbing fact of the matter is—they do know something. Most of what they say is outright lies—like I've cheated on Isabel before, that I got out of the restaurant business because it was going bankrupt—but there are some truths.

It's the truth that is the most damaging.

It is the truth about Vera.

The article explains how the "anonymous" source had suspicions about her, thinking she was nothing more than a "Canadian refugee," and looked into her situation. She was able to obtain that Vera was in the country thanks to a work permit through Las Palabras, but she had been recently fired, and would have to leave the country soon or risk deportation.

I don't panic. I don't lose it. I merely drive the car away from the stadium and head straight to Isabel's. I don't care about work. I don't honk at the traffic. It's like I'm purely on auto-pilot now, heading toward the only place I know that I can get answers.

I don't know what I'm going to say or what I'm going to do. Because of this source, someone I know that's related to Isabel if not Isabel herself, Vera can no longer hide until January. She will have to leave. Unless she finds a new job and new sponsorship in a week—and she hasn't really been looking since we've been under house arrest—she is gone.

It is the worst case scenario and it is real.

I pull the car up to the house and run to the door. This time I don't knock, and as I barge in the unlocked house, I see dear Chloe Ann, dressed in all pink and watching TV.

"Daddy!" she cries out, and runs over to give me a hug.

"Hello, my darling," I tell her, and squeeze her tighter than ever.

"Are you here to play with me?" she asks.

"I wish I was," I say. "I can't stay long, and I have to speak with your mother. How about you go up to your room for a little bit?"

"Why?"

I look at her with pleading eyes. "Please, Chloe Ann," I implore just as Isabel comes out of the kitchen, wiping her hands on a dishtowel. She does not seem surprised to see me.

"Mama," Chloe Ann says, looking to her.

Isabel hesitates then nods. "Go to your room now. This will only take a moment."

Like hell it will.

Chloe Ann pouts but runs up the stairs to her room anyway. When we hear the door shut, Isabel turns to face me.

"What do you want, Mateo?"

"What do you think? How about we cut the charades and you tell me exactly what I read today in Caliente." I'm so angry that I'm shocked I'm able to form words, to sound so cool and collected. I feel anything but.

"I don't know what you're talking about," she says, and turns, walking into the kitchen.

I follow, undeterred. "You do. Was it you? Are you feeling guilty that you have to lie about it to me? Haven't you lied enough already?"

She stares at me, face expressionless, and I continue. "I can read the article out loud to you if you want, but I know you've already read it. So who was it? You? Are you that desperate to get me?"

When she still doesn't say anything, I can't help but raise my voice. "Answer me!" I demand. "Tell me who spread the lies, who talked?"

She tosses the towel on the counter then turns around, leaning back against it, and folds her arms. The kitchen gleams beside her, as sterile as she is. Finally she says, "I didn't see any lies. Especially not about Vera. That was all the truth—isn't it?"

"Who did it?" I repeat.

"Why does it matter?"

"Was it you?"

"I wish it was," she says snidely. "But I didn't want to be the one to stoop to your level."

"I defended you!" I cry out, suddenly overwhelmed by the rage burning through me, making my skin hot, seared, inflamed.

She gives me an incredulous look and brushes her blonde hair behind her ears in such a slow, easy manner that it only fuels my inner fire. "When have you *ever* defended me?" she says.

My mouth opens. Closes. She's trying to discredit our whole marriage; she's trying to put the noose around my neck and pull me into years of hidden wars and secret tallies and a million cards held close to the chest. I can't go down that path; I'll never get out alive.

I suck in my breath and try to control my temper. She's provoking me. She's doing a good job, she always has. "In the lobby of my apartment," I tell her, hoping that the emphasis on *my* burns like a pepper. "You went after Vera—spat on her. You were about to fight her. I defended you when she fought back."

Her eyes narrow, and I see it was a mistake to say this; it was a mistake to defend her. "And why did you defend me?"

"Because you're the mother of my child," I tell her. "Because you were still family. Because I was at fault, Vera was at fault, and you had every right to be upset. I defended you because I thought it was the right thing to do."

"And now?" she asks breezily, her penciled brow cocked.

My jaw feels so tense I have to wiggle it back and forth before I can even answer. "Now I wish I hadn't. You'll no longer get any sympathy from me, and I will no longer feel guilty for what I did."

Her upper lip curls, about to shoot something venomous my way, but I raise my hand in the air to stop her and take a step forward. "Don't let what I did make you this person. Don't let your fucking family think you belong at their level."

Isabel's face is the blank face of a glacier. Cold, impassive, smooth, and with miles buried underneath. "You should be nicer to me, Mateo. I already told you that before, didn't I?" There is nothing but threat in her voice, and it isn't empty.

"Getting Vera deported isn't going to stop anything," I tell her. "It won't bring you and I back together. It won't stop me from loving her."

At that, she lets out a derisive snort. "This was never about love, Mateo."

"If you had ever loved me, you would understand."

My words hang between us like smoke in a dirty bar. I don't need to hear that she loved me, that our marriage wasn't just a sham for the wrong reasons, that she once believed I was her world. I don't need to hear it, but I want to hear it. I want to know that my life before this wasn't a lie, I want to know that Chloe Ann was conceived out of love.

"I never loved you," she says, and those words join the others until it's all I can do to breathe.

But it's fine. "Well, I did love you, Isabel."

"And then it just stopped."

I nod. "Sometimes love just stops," I say. "Sometimes it needs to be fed."

I hope I'm getting through to her. I'm being as sincere as I can while trying to control my temper, the helpless rage that has its hold. I don't think I was ever so open during our marriage. But I can see the ice in her eyes, the strain on her lips. She's not taking it in. She's not listening.

"All that needed feeding was your dick," she says. "So you pushed me aside for someone who would do it, someone younger, trashier. You thought it would be fun to get with some diseased whore. Let's really stick it to Isabel."

I can't listen to this anymore. Not from her, not from anyone. Vera is a modern witch that everyone keeps wanting to burn at the stake, and every time she catches fire, I do too. I close my eyes and try to compose myself.

"You just wanted to fuck this little bitch, bet she's constantly sucking men off when you aren't looking. Younger, better men than you."

Breathe in. Breathe out. Ignore the crushing pain, the anger.

She just wants to get to you.

I breathe in sharply through my nose. "When did you let hate take over your soul?" I ask her, trying to keep my voice calm. "When did you stop being the person I used to know?"

"When you fucked her and fucked up my life," she says, words sharp as knives, and I can hear her step toward me. She's right in my face but I refuse to open my eyes, to acknowledge her. "You've ruined everything I worked so hard for. Everything." She smells like gin, and the scent dissolves as I hear her walk across the kitchen to the door leading to the backyard.

The door opens and I hold my breath.

"And I will never, ever let you forget it, Mateo," she says before she shuts the door behind her.

When I open my eyes, I am pitching left toward the wall, and my arm can barely hold me up. I feel like there are bats in my ribcage, caught between my heart and my lungs in a flurry of violent, black wings.

All at once I know I'm going to lose Vera.

It feels like I might lose the sun from the sky.

After I leave Isabel's, I go back into work. I haven't heard from Vera yet which means she hasn't seen that particular magazine. I have this urge to keep the news from her if I can, and I hope that I can still whisk her off to San Sebastian for the weekend. Though I would be burdened with guilt, she would be saved from it, at least for a few days. We deserve this. She deserves it most of all.

But first I have to deal with Pedro. He calls me into his office just after noon for another talk, and I'm starting to think this will forever be a weekly thing. Find something about Mateo to complain about, call him in, threaten him with one thing or another, and then offer him a cigar.

Pedro is obviously just as obsessed with the tabloids as I am because the magazine is open on his desk when I come in.

He's calm, which I guess is a good sign, though things could go either way. He asks me who the informant is. I tell him I don't know—which is the truth—but that I suspect Isabel's family. They've always been a pack of vultures, vying for the spotlight and the privileges they think are owed to them by blood. It could be her cold-hearted mother or her conniving sister or social climbing brother. The whole family is interchangeable, and in the end it doesn't seem to matter. Whoever the anonymous source was, they wanted to rake me through the coals, and they did.

In short, Pedro tells me he doesn't know what to do with me, and part of me is tempted to tell him what to do with himself. I care enough about how things seem, how things are, and I don't need to hear it from my boss.

"Why don't you just make Warren the coach and fire me?" I ask him, feeling bold, with nothing to lose. "That way you don't have to deal with this problem again."

He finally looks shocked. "Is that what you think?" he asks. "That I would fire you over this?"

I nod. "Yes, I do. You've called me in here enough over this, something that is more or less out of my hands. I do think you'd fire me over it. But here, let me give you an easy way out of it. If you think I'm going to choose between being with Vera or being on Atlético again, I will walk away from you. I don't need this job, but I do need her."

He purses his lips, looking down at the magazine with raised brows. "I must say," he says, "I didn't really expect to hear that."

I get out of my chair and stare down at him. "Well, you've heard it. You may think you know me, Mr. del Torro, but you don't. Everyone makes these opinions about me based on what they've seen and heard from other people and other sources, but the only way you'll ever know the real me is if you watch what I do and listen to what I say. I am happy to be back on the team, and in time I think I could help shape these boys into something even more spectacular than what they are. I have that faith in myself, confidence in my skills, and I know a good thing when I see it. But Vera is a good thing too, better than all the rest. And when it comes down to the things that matter the most in my life, she trumps everything. So shit articles and idle threats and unfair expectations don't really amount to much when it comes to my life because I already know what's important—and what's not."

I go for the door, and before I leave I give him a cordial nod. "Have a good weekend."

After that exit, I feel alive with energy. The adrenaline is going crazy through my system, holding me on the edge of shame and euphoria. On the way to the apartment I call Vera and tell her to pack her bags, that we're leaving for San Sebastian immediately. She seems caught off-guard by my impulsiveness but happy about it, and on that alone I know she hasn't seen the magazine yet.

"Is Chloe Ann able to make it?" she asks.

"No," I tell her, "but it's okay. It will just be us. We need it."

There are no arguments there.

Two hours later we are in the SUV and halfway to the seaside city, stopping at farm stands to snack on fresh tomatoes and cheese. Vera seems to shine brighter than the sun; the claustrophobic smog and heat and people of Madrid want to be just a memory.

But it's not to me. I keep the big, bad truth from her, keep it close to me like a knife, dangerous to the both of us. I try and split my mind into two and ignore our reality, the one that's closing in on us, closer and closer. I know that by Monday Vera will know. Even if she never sees her face in it—which seems impossible—I know I have to tell her. She has to know that she's leaving.

"Are you okay?" she asks me as we climb back in the car. Waving fields of sunflowers dance in the warm breeze on either side of the highway.

I manage to smile. "Yes, I'm fine." But it's nearly impossible to fake it. The future looms, weighted in my heart. I can't lose her, I can't lose her, I can't lose her.

What can I do?

When we get to San Sebastian, the air is whipped by sprays of salt water, and we check into a quaint little hotel on the western edge of the sandy Bahia de La Concha. It's private and romantic, and the old lady who works behind the front desk seems oblivious to everything except our comfort.

Our room looks right across the bay, the waves of the Atlantic rolling in with the sunset shining on their crests. We change into comfortable clothes and head down the street to a little English fish and chip shop that we saw. We get a bunch of it wrapped in greasy newspapers, tiny packets of vinegar and ketchup, grab a bottle of red wine from a depot, and then head down to the beach.

It is still light out though the sun is long gone and the sky is the color of periwinkles in spring. Tiny white dots pop out in the blue, stars coming to shine. The sound of the waves is soothing, and even though there are people on the beach still, particularly some homeless people camped out in sleeping bags at one end, it feels like the whole place is just for us.

Vera licks the grease and vinegar off her fingers then lies back in the sand. She closes her eyes and breathes in deeply for a beat or two, then she tilts her head and looks at me.

"Lie back with me. Let's have a siesta," she says, patting the sand beside her.

I lean back, my head nestled into the grains that are still warm from the heat of the day. I grab her hand and hold on tight as we watch the sky darken and the constellations come into view. Like old times, I ask her to tell me the stories behind each one, and she does so. There is love in her voice, maybe for me, maybe for the stars themselves, and I am so overcome with everything that a single tear manages to escape my eye and slides down the corner of my cheek.

It's dark and as such, she can't see it. She just goes on, telling me once again about mythic beasts and stories of hope and love. I am sure half of them are made up just from her imagination, and it only serves to remind me how wonderful, bright, and charming she is. I wish that her Spanish was good enough so that she could share the same stories with Chloe Ann, then I wish that she'll one day share the same with a child of our own.

But how can any of that be now, now that the world is poised to take her away. Going back to Canada will ruin Vera, drive the life right out of her. Though times here have been hard, she still has determination, the verve to face her challenges, to want to change things when she feels trapped. When she's faced against her family, she shrinks and becomes less of the woman than she is. I don't want that to happen to her, and that is my most unselfish thought.

My most selfish thought is that I won't survive without her by my side. I need her to stay because it's the only way I know how to live now. I can't go back to just being me—it has to be the both of us. We were worth every sacrifice, every burnt bridge. We need each other more than we need the hearts pumping in our chests.

How could so much have changed so fast? I grip her hand even tighter, wishing I could sink down into the sand, let the beach swallow us whole, and take her with me. I want to shelter her from what's coming, and it rips my soul apart knowing that I can't.

"Mateo," she says softly, but I can't bear to turn my head to look at her. I want to keep feeling her, staring at the stars. I don't want her to see the pain in my eyes. I don't want to ruin our night.

"Yes," I answer, just as softly. I stare up and see a shooting star dart across the sky. I close my eyes and make a wish.

I want Vera with me forever.

"I love you, you know," she says, and it's enough to make me open my eyes.

I swallow hard, so afraid I'm going to crack. I pull her hand to my lips and kiss her palm. "I love you, too."

"Do you think," she says, then trails off. She sighs and it sounds like her heart is heavy. "Do you think that we'll get a happily ever after, after all of this?"

Her question stuns me so much that I have no choice but to look at her. Her eyes are dark, wet pools, the distant streetlights reflecting in them.

"Of course we will," I say. "What makes you say that?"

"Because you don't sound convinced."

I rub my lips together, trying to think, trying to sound convinced enough to her. "Vera, my Estrella, I want us together forever. I want us to be happy. I want a lot of things that fools can only dream of."

"And you think we are fools?"

"I think we are fools if we don't dream."

"But wanting is not the same as knowing, as having. Do you think we're going to be okay?"

I want to lie to her but I can't. I let out a low breath and say, "I think we deserve to be okay. But in the short term…"

"You know something," she says. "Don't you?"

I glance at her, frowning. "Why makes you say that?"

She gathers sand and lets it fall through her fingers, watching the grains absently as she repeats the action over and over. "I've been with you for over a year, and in that time we've been through a lot. I knew you after a month at Las Palabras. I definitely know you now. I know when you're hurting, when you're troubled. You think you can hide everything away beneath your beautiful face and your classy gestures, but I know the real you. And I know there is something going on right now, something that's breaking your heart." She pauses and swallows loudly. She blinks a few times, her eyes growing wetter, and that heart of mine that she's talking about, I can feel the deep pinch. "I'm afraid to know what it is because I know it's going to break my heart too. But please, Mateo. I need to know. I can't let you go through this alone. Let me in with you."

I lean over and kiss her lips, taste the tears that have spilled down her cheeks. I feel so much love for her and so much fucking sorrow that I can't even separate the two. I push my fingers through the silky wildness of her hair and hold her in place, as if I can hold her here forever.

It is a beautiful kiss. It is the one that precedes sadness and change, the last one that feels strong and free. I relish it, relish her. When I pull away from her lips and mouth and tongue and soul, I will have to tell her the truth. I will have to destroy her, destroy this, destroy me.

It is the pain that makes me pull apart. Everything has already changed inside.

"Vera," I say quietly, trailing my fingers down the smoothness of her forehead, the ski-jump of her nose, the fullness of lips I was feeling just moments ago. "We've been found out. It is no longer a secret that you don't have another work permit. You're going to have to leave in a week."

A shudder runs through her, as if she's cold, but I think it's shock and fear clashing together in the most horrific way. Her eyes grow large and the world grows smaller.

"How did that happen?" she whispers. I exhale through my nose, gathering strength, and tell her the ugly truth of what I saw that morning.

She immediately gets to her feet and starts marching hurriedly across the sand. I have to spring up, stepping on the leftover fish and chips in my haste to run after her.

"Where are you going?" I ask, grabbing her by the arm and pulling her toward me.

She looks crazed, a feral creature caught in a snare. "I have to see the magazine!"

"No, Vera," I tell her, holding her tight even though she tries to rip away. "It won't help anything."

"I have to leave you!" she screams at me. It echoes across the beach, across the waves, across the sky.

"I know," I say, because I do know. There is no happily ever after for right now. There is no hint at a future. There is only what we know, that she has to leave me and that we'll both be nothing without each other. "I know. I'm sorry."

Her face crumples and she lets out a sob that has her doubling over. She nearly drops to her knees, crying out in pain, and I hold her up, hold her to me. She sobs into my chest, her back shaking, and I am so close to letting go and collapsing with her. I have to be strong, I have to be, but it's harder than I ever thought it would be. The world has hurled so many knives my way, but this is the one that makes me want to fall.

"I'm so sorry," I say again, cradling her to me, even though I know that saying sorry won't help anything. "I didn't want to tell you. I wanted this to be our last weekend together before the truth set in. I wanted us to be like we were when we were free."

"We were never free," she says, voice muffled, but she grasps my shirt with her hands like she's afraid to let go. I'm afraid to let go, too.

"No, I suppose we weren't. But at least we were together."

Silence passes between us. Waves crash. People in the distance laugh at some joke. A car honks its horn. The world is going on like normal, oblivious to the world that is ending on the beach.

Chapter Ten

"Two medium coffees to go please," I tell the surly looking barista at the café. After I pay, I turn and lean against the counter and look for Vera. She's in a souvenir shop across the street, perusing the gaudy racks for some sort of reminder of Spain. I told her there is time for that in Madrid, but she seems to think there is no time left at all and this may be the only chance she has, here in San Sebastian.

I wish I could say she is wrong, but she's isn't. There really is no time. Tomorrow we will return to Madrid and she will start the process of finding her way home. Of course I will buy her flight. She is adamant that she can afford it, that she has some money saved up, but I have seen the ATM receipts, and I know two hundred dollars wouldn't even get her halfway there.

There is some sort of irony in the fact that I am buying yet another ticket for her to go back to Vancouver. One might joke that I'm constantly trying to send her away, but it's nothing to laugh at. It's everything to rage at, yell at, to cry at. I've been wanting to do nothing but fight against life, but ever since I told Vera the truth—and after she saw it in the magazine for herself—she shut down and succumbed to it. She's accepted it.

I won't. I can't. I just don't know how to fight. I don't know how to get what I want.

I just want Vera. I want her by my side. I want her with me. I just want her. I have so much that I can have, so much that I don't need, but in the end I just want *her*.

Why does such a need have to be so hard?

When I get the coffees, I walk across the street to join her. She shows me the Spain magnets and pens and t-shirts and bookmarks she's snapped up. It's all junk. But in her desperate hands, she clutches them like forgotten treasures.

We get in the SUV and drive. That was our plan for the day, just to drive and drive and drive and feel free for the last time. No rules, no boundaries, no borders. The drive takes us northeast along the coast until we cross into France. Why not?

"Ever been to France?" I ask her, and for the first time that day, a natural smile appears on her face.

"No," she says. "Are we in France?"

I nod. "Yes. And I know just where to take you. Biarritz."

"Sounds . . . ritzy."

"Like fancy? It kind of is. But it's very nice. Perfect for a day trip."

I haven't been to Biarritz for a very long time, but as we park and make our way along the seaside walk with its stunning views of the beachside city, sloping hills of white-washed, shuttered buildings, and crashing surf, it seems nothing has changed. The town is a wonderful mix of wealthy vacationers and surfers here to catch the area's famous waves. Some people could be both.

The path takes us out briefly on the promenade, giving us a panoramic view of the town and the ocean and the dramatic coastline, to the end, the rock of the Virgin Mary. The white statue stares down at us, as if asking us for forgiveness, yet as Vera and I hold on to each other, we feel we are the ones asking her. We are the sinners here. And now we are paying for it.

The melancholy follows us around like ocean mist, and few words are spoken between us. There isn't much to say, and yet there is too much to say. We make our way past picturesque restaurants, their windows lined with hanging vines of dried garlic and chili peppers as red as blood, and past small boats, sheltered in tiny, enclosed marinas, walls of stone the only barrier between the raging sea outside.

While we walk, I hear the faint sound of music. It is a saxophone—not my most favorite of instruments—but here it is melodic, sad, and powerful. It rises over the sea at us and bathes us like the sun.

I squeeze Vera's hand and she squeezes back. We both hear it, we both feel it. It's almost like a swan song just for us, something conjured up by the stars, or God, or the Virgin Mary herself. It is only when we turn the corner that we see the source.

There is a rocky outcrop sticking out into the surf, and at the very end of the promenade is a lone street musician. He is playing to no one but the ocean, and the sounds of the saxophone seem even sadder this way.

"Vera," I find myself saying, unable to stop the emotion that's trying to claw its way out of my chest. I stop, pulling her to the side of the path, the waves crashing below us, and hold her sweet face in my hands. Bronze and white. So beautiful together.

"Vera," I say again, staring hard and long into her searching eyes, and I don't try to fight it anymore. "Vera, will you marry me?"

My words have taken her by surprise. They have taken me by surprise. But that doesn't stop it from being the most real, honest, and raw thing I've ever said.

Her mouth goes into that pretty *O* shape, and her eyebrows come together, and her eyes are dancing like she's in love. In this moment I am a man of hope and potential; I have been given a glimpse of the person I will become, someone to do her proud. Someone better.

But the moment is lost when her face crumples into everything that is sadness and heartache. It is not the face I wanted at all. It is not her hand, it is not her heart. It is only her mind, wanting to push me back.

"Oh, Mateo," she says breathlessly. "No."

And just like that, I feel as if I really have lost everything. I am rejected. I will not have her as my wife, the mother of my children, or anything else I have dreamed of having, like the fool that I am.

I have nothing.

I suddenly gasp, realizing I can barely breathe. "No?" I repeat, just to make sure.

She shakes her head and tears spill down her cheeks. "I can't. Not like this, not this way."

"What way?" I ask, pained. My hand is at my heart now because I fear it may stop working. Maybe I welcome it.

"This way!" she cries, throwing her hands out to the side, instantly volatile. "You're only asking me as a means to stay."

Now it's my turn to be shocked. "What? Wait a minute. Please, Vera, that is not what is going on here."

"Yes it is!"

I grab her by the shoulders and hold her, wishing I could shake some sense into her. "No. No. I have wanted to ask you for a very long time now. This has nothing to do with trying to keep you in the country."

"I'll still have to leave," she says feebly.

"Do you hear me?" I say again, louder now because I feel like I'm splintering and no one will ever hear from me again. "I have always wanted to marry you. I want you to be the mother of my children."

"We've never even discussed children!" she cries out, alarmed. "You don't even know if I want them."

This is true but I can't feel ashamed about it. "I know, I figured we would talk about it along the way. You do want kids, don't you?"

She shrugs helplessly. "I don't know. Maybe. It's nothing I really think about. I've been so busy just trying to stay here each fucking day."

And I am hit with our age difference again. It has been something I've thought about often, no matter our circumstances. She's too young to have it on her brain all the time. Perhaps she's just the type of girl to never have it on her brain at all. Either one wouldn't surprise me, and yet I would love either one just the same.

I look away, turning to face the street musician who is still playing his sad song. I feel like it could be about me, the man who once had everything and nothing at the same time.

I feel her hand on my shoulder, light and tentative.

"Look, Mateo," she says quietly. "It's just too much. I can't deal with this, I can't handle it. Not now. Any other time, any other way, maybe I would have said yes."

"Maybe," I mumble, not turning around.

"Do you even have a ring?"

I sigh. "No," I say harshly, frustrated. "Lucia wanted to come with me when it came time to pick it out."

There is a pause. "Oh. You talked about this with Lucia?"

I nod. "Si."

She is silent. She takes her hand away. I continue to stare at the sea, contemplating how cold the water is and whether it would shock me if I jumped in. A body can only take so much shock. I wonder how much I can take.

"I'm sorry," she says. "I just . . . it's not right. It doesn't feel right. I can only go by how I feel."

"If you weren't leaving," I ask her. "Would you have said yes?"

She hesitates then says, "I don't know."

"You know, by pushing me away like this, you aren't making things any easier on yourself. It will still hurt when you leave."

"I know."

I slowly turn around and look at her. I just can't accept it. "Why won't you marry me? What happened to our happily ever after?"

She looks like a broken woman. "I never said there was one."

"But don't you want there to be?"

She looks at her red toenails peeking out from her sandals. "I just want you, Mateo."

It feels like she's just reaching into my chest now and squeezing every last drop out of me. "And I want you."

She shuts her eyes as if she's in pain. "And yet we don't have much choice. Whether you mean what you are asking me or you're doing it to make me stay, it doesn't matter. I'll always wonder if it was real or not. And marriage—you of all people should know—is a big, big thing. Yes, I think I'm young. Yes, I don't know if I want kids yet or not. I think I do. But all that aside, it's not something I'm afraid of—as long as it's for the right reasons. And right now, I fear the reasons you are asking me. You may even be tricking yourself. So I can't say yes, even though it is something I've dreamed about too—Mrs. Mateo Casalles. I've always thought it sounded so beautiful, almost as beautiful as waking up to you every morning for the rest of my life. But life has other plans for us. It always does."

"You're breaking me," I tell her in a ragged whisper.

A tear rolls down her cheek and she doesn't bother to wipe it away. "And I'm already broken."

I grab her hand and pull her close to me. I wipe away her tear with my thumb, so gently, so as not to break her further. "I won't let this be the end of us."

She tries to smile. "I believe you."

"Do you really?" I ask, kissing her softly on the cheek. "Do you really believe what I am telling you is true? Do you really believe I'll fight for you?"

Her eyes dart to the side but she won't find any answers out there. They all lie in me; they are all there if she wants them.

"It's getting late," she says, rubbing her hands up and down her arms as if she's cold. "Shouldn't we head back to San Sebastian?"

The sun is hours from hitting the horizon. What she really wants is to escape this conversation. I should want the same, to run away from a rejected proposal. But I don't want that. I want to stay and talk. I want to see that fire in her, that urge to run headfirst into battle. It's like the concept of going back home has already changed her, compromised her, and she's resigned to become the person she used to be.

I can't let that happen, I won't let that happen. But beyond feeling and thinking that, there is nothing I can do. I can only be there for her, no matter how badly my heart is breaking, no matter how soft and bruised my ego has become.

I take hold of her arm and say, "Okay. We can go back."

But we can't go back, not to the place we once were, where we once were free.

When we arrive back in Madrid on Sunday afternoon, we are both surprised to feel the difference. The temperature in the city seems to have cooled down by at least ten degrees. The temperature between us seems to have done the same.

Vera is definitely trying to push me away, and I'm trying to pull her in, and we're going nowhere. She talks to her mother, her brother, even her father. Her mother had told her when she first decided to move to Spain that she wasn't welcome in the house anymore. Vera is worried she has no place to go.

200

As if things can't get any harder for her.

Thankfully, she has a good brother who convinces her mother to let her stay, at least for a little bit. Vera is now torn between starting a life in Vancouver and moving to the province of Alberta to be with her father and stepmom. I am torn between letting her go and fighting for her to stay.

The fight is futile, but I try.

She leaves in two days, and Pedro is nice enough to let me have work off to spend time with her. To his credit, he doesn't seem smug about the fact that Vera has to leave. In fact, everyone at Atlético feels sorry for me. I'm not sure if I like the sympathy. Sometimes I think I would rather have their disgust again. Somehow it was more manageable and easier to bear.

The night before she is to leave, I find Vera sitting on the balcony, drinking wine, lost in thought. I am hit with the greatest sense of loss I have ever known, like I'm about to lose some driving force inside me that keeps me alive. It's almost hard to breathe, and I know she'll take the air and sun and stars with her when she goes.

She's going.

She's leaving.

She's leaving me.

The pain is debilitating.

I lean against the side of the glass door and watch her. She knows I'm there but she doesn't turn around to see. So I watch her, soak her in, this memory of her. I'm afraid now that this is the only thing I'll remember, the sight of her alone, her features deadened with despair, the night spread out before her echoing our loneliness.

Somehow I manage to clear my throat, find my voice, and ask, "I thought you were going out for a good-bye dinner with Claudia."

She takes a moment before she finally turns to look at me. "I'd rather spend my last night with you. My last night . . ."

Her voice breaks over the last word. She's been so strong, or maybe just so numb, for the past few days that to hear the damage nearly brings me to my knees.

I choke back on everything. Words, tears, wishes. I choke back on everything but love.

I cross the balcony in two strides. I collapse to my knees beside her, wrapping my arms around her waist and burying my head in her chest. A cry rolls out of her body, anguished, panicked, the epitome of sorrow, and when it grows louder, I realize that it's coming from me too.

It hurts deeper than any wound, something festering from the inside out. And still I can't wrap my head around what this means. My heart and soul seem to know, from the way I'm holding on to her, from the way she's holding on to me. But I can't imagine how tomorrow I'll drop her off at the airport and that will be the end of it.

The end of us.

But it can't be the end. It doesn't have to be the end. I had told Vera that she would only have to return to Canada for a few months, then, if she could get into school—which never seems to be a problem if you have the money—she could return in January, safe and legal.

Without all the plans though, all the hopes, it still feels like this is the end. Once she steps back on her home soil, I'm afraid all that we've been through, all that we are, will disappear into the atmosphere.

"I don't think I can do it again," she sobs quietly, her hands nestled in my hair. "I don't think I can leave you again. It almost destroyed me before. Those were the hardest months of my entire life."

"But at least you know you can return," I tell her, still mumbling into the softness of her chest. It feels so much like home. "We're different, better people than we were back then. There was no certainty then like there is now."

"There is never any certainty," she spits out.

I raise my head slowly to look at her. The world seems to spin. "What do you mean?"

She looks away, anguished. "You know what I mean. Five months is a long time. What if you fall in love with someone else?"

"What if you fall in love with someone else?"

"I won't."

"How do I know that?" I ask, and look away as if I am ashamed. "Usually when a man proposes and the woman says no, things don't—how do you say, bode well?—for the situation."

She shakes her head once. "It's not like that."

"So we're not over."

"We've never been over." She places her hand on my heart. "Not here. Just because I said no . . . Mateo, you know why I said it. It doesn't mean what you think it does. It's more of a not yet. But . . ." She looks away. "Because I said no, I'm worried you'll start looking elsewhere. For someone who will say yes."

"No," I tell her adamantly.

"How can I know? How will we know?"

I place my fingers under her chin and tip her face toward me. "I won't. Look at me. Look at me, my Estrella. Don't you know what that means? You're my star. How many people on this earth have their own star? And you shine just for me. How could anyone else ever compare to this?"

I hoist myself up so that I'm leaning over her, and I stare down into her yearning eyes. She wants to believe me. She *has* to believe me.

I kiss her lips, so satiny soft that they threaten to unravel me all over again. "You are my everything," I say, lips moving against hers. "I've said it before and I will say it again, and I'll go to my grave saying it. You are my star, my light, my love. And it doesn't matter if you believe in it or not because it is the truth and the truth always finds a way to shine."

She doesn't say anything for a moment, but then she answers in her own way. She kisses me with strength and fire, enough to catch me off-guard. Her passion is on her sleeve, and in our mouths, and in the heat of our fingers as they grip each other tightly.

Just when I'm about to take her clothes off right there, she whispers, hushed and hoarse, "I love you," and

I know that this requires delicacy. There should be nothing fast and frantic about our last night together. It should be slow, languid, decadent. It should feel like the night burns into day and burns into night again. It should be long enough to make a million memories.

I stand up and then scoop her into in my arms like I'm some kind of hero. Only I'm no hero. I'm just a man in love.

Though there's never been anything more courageous than loving someone.

I take her down the hallway to the bedroom, throw back the sheets, and place her on the bed, where she lies beneath me, waiting. I straddle her, my thighs on either side of her hips, and reach down to ever so slowly push the straps of her dress off her shoulders, and leave soft kisses in their place. She tastes sweeter than wine and I run my tongue over her skin, feeling it awaken under my touch.

She reaches for my zipper but I gently nudge her back. "Slowly, slowly," I tell her in Spanish. "We make love slowly, as it prolongs the night."

More than that, it prolongs *us*.

I peel the top of her dress down her body, all the way to her stomach, and her nipples harden, exposed to my hungry eyes. I immediately dip my head and lick them softly until she groans, arching her back. She is so perfect, the feel of her, the shape, the way her body responds to my every move.

I can't believe I have to say goodbye to this.

It hits me hard again, an aftershock. I clench my eyes shut and will it away. I can't think like this, not now.

Vera runs her fingers through my hair, slowly, keeping with the rhythm, the act that we have all the time in the world.

I tease her breasts from the soft outer swell to the nipple and back again, flicking them like I'm trying to lap up the rest of the richest dessert. Sometimes I think she can have an orgasm just from me giving her breasts extra attention, and I'm wondering if I should attempt this tonight. It may be our last chance; it would be another way to get the most out of each other, another memory.

The way her fingers are digging into my skull tells me that she's getting restless, that she wants nothing more than my tongue between her legs, to have me inside her bringing her relief. She will get her relief, more than once.

I continue to work at her breasts, licking a warm path up the swollen corners toward the middle. I gently nip at her, bringing in sharp bursts of pain with the soothing stroke of my tongue, alternating the two until she begins squirming beneath me, her face contorted with that anguished need for both more and less.

"Mateo," she groans, her fingers tightening their grip. "Come inside me."

I reach up with my hand and place it over her mouth. "Shhhh," I tell her. "Let me do this for you."

She resigns and leans further back into the bed. I take my mouth and place it flush over her peaks, sucking them gently and working them with my tongue. I lap and flick, my attention completely on her, trying to make her eyes roll back, her thighs shudder.

"Mateo," she groans again, pulling on my hair now. "I can't . . ."

But I persist. Her breathing deepens, then sharpens, hot and heavy pants that inflame my own desire. I give and give until she's writhing beneath me and yanking my hair with all her strength. I squeeze her breasts, bite her nipples, and it's enough to cause her body to quake uncontrollably. Breathless words come from her open, yearning mouth, wild and animalistic.

Then her tremors slow and her body relaxes into the mattress.

"Oh my god," she says, her head rolling back and forth, her wide eyes staring at the ceiling. "Oh my god, oh my god."

"Keep saying my name, it's fine," I tell her, unable to stop from grinning. I feel an incredible sense of pride to leave this mark on her. It feels wonderful to feel this even if it's just temporary, just for tonight.

"It's like you can put your tongue anywhere and I'm coming just like that. Fuck, me," she says, sounding amazed. "I didn't even think that was possible."

"I think with you, anything is possible." I sit up and unbutton my shirt before discarding it behind me. She reaches up and runs her fingers over my muscles, that hunger still in her eyes, but it's not just for me, it's for us and everything that we are. She's come so alive in this relationship, and so have I. It feeds us, makes us stronger, better.

I kiss her, her lips richer than honeycomb, and quickly remove my clothes until we are both naked beside each other. I stare into her eyes, my hands trailing up and down the soft slopes of her body, my fingers circling the inky constellations on her skin, as if her skin itself could tell me their stories. I close my eyes and commit the feeling of her to memory, wishing I too could be embedded on her skin, that she could never shed me.

Vera places her finger beneath my eyes and I am surprised to feel her wipe away a tear. I must be crying just a bit.

She murmurs something then kisses me with salt and flavor, and I move my body on top of hers. My fingers skip down her stomach and hips and settle in between her thighs. She is still wet and warm from her previous orgasm, and she feels like home. I slide my fingers along her slickness and up inside her, rubbing against her G-spot with even pressure.

I love the way her body gives into my hands, like I can mold her into anything I want. But all I want is her, forever in my bed, just like this, her passion awoken by mine again and again. She arches her back, knees coming up to give me better access, and I slip my fingers out and position my cock there instead.

I push in deliberately, inch by inch, and let the sensation flood through me. This is so beautiful and so final. My eyes close, and when I go deep, as far as I can go inside of her, it feels like we are one and will stay one and nothing will pull us apart.

My feelings are lies, but they will do for now.

I have to control myself so I will not come before we are both ready. Even if we were both ready, I wouldn't want this to be over so fast. I breathe in deeply with each slow, wet thrust.

"How do I feel?" I ask her, my voice richer, darker, wrapped up in desire. "Because you feel like the heavens."

She grins lazily, her eyes closed. "You feel like Mateo."

"And this is good, yes?" I drive myself in deeper, and she lets out a moan.

She opens her lustful eyes to stare up at me. "Yes," she says breathlessly. "The best I'll ever have."

A lump forms in my throat, and I quickly swallow it down. She will also be the best I'll ever have, and I may never have her again.

I push through the pain. It is the only way out. I fuck her faster now but still in control, desperate to drive away the sorrow that's waiting beyond, wanting to just feel this way and nothing else, but not wanting to rush. It is push and pull, and everything inside me is building, building, building until I am on the edge and so is she.

I am so afraid to let go.

"Mateo," she whispers, lips at my ear. "I can't hold back any longer."

A shudder rolls down my back and I still myself, unable to keep going without losing it. Sweat pools between our overheated bodies, our hands gliding over each other, yearning to hold on. I am determined but so is she. She reaches behind to play with my ass, and she knows how much that drives me wild.

Everything she does drives me wild.

And now I can't hold back anymore either.

I reach the crescendo and come so hard into her that it feels like the room shakes and I lose all control. I am brought to another place—a place that I can only find deep inside her body—and it is this other world of light and stars and beauty. I am calling out her name, vaguely aware of how loud I am, how powerful my groans are, how concisely this pleasure rips me apart. She is a mixture of nails in my back and frantic gasps that echo throughout the room. She pulses around me and we both keep coming, and for one gorgeous moment I think we will come forever.

But it eventually leaves us and it leaves us bereft. I collapse on top of her, nearly crushing her, and I bury my face in her neck, holding on to her limbs and trying to breathe, trying to keep her. I'm not sure if I even have a pulse anymore, if I am even Mateo Casalles. I'm not sure if she's really real beneath me, hot and wet and shaking. She is crying and I am crying, and it doesn't seem fair that this is what we are and what we are no longer permitted to be.

All at once I know that if Vera and I never see each other again, I will still go on and find happiness because now I know what it looks like. Now I know what it feels like. My eyes have been opened forever, and if I had never been so lucky to have her in my life, I would have never lived.

"I'll forever keep searching for you," I murmur. "I will look up to the sky and let it point me your way. I will not let you go, Vera. I will never let you go."

She sobs quietly in response, and I can feel how much this is breaking her. It's like we're the only thing keep each other together.

I kiss her lips, her nose, her forehead, smoothing her hair back with my hands. "I will never let you go," I repeat.

I stay inside of her for as long as I can.

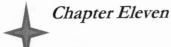

Chapter Eleven

Vera's flight is at one in the afternoon, and even though I want nothing more than to spend our last hours in bed, our bodies entwined forever, there is far too much to do. Claudia and Ricardo come by before they are off to work, and I have to leave the apartment to get some coffee because my heart can't take any more tears. Vera has made an impact on these people and they are hurting just as much as I am to see her go.

The drive to the airport goes by too quickly. The last time we went, the future was full of such promise. We were heading to Canada with our friends. Now only she is going, and I am starting to lose faith in her return. If I could, I would manipulate planes and move mountains, but I can only go so far as she will let me. She has to want to return to me.

Return to me.

The words catch in the whirlwind of my mind, tugging at my heart.

Return to me, my star.

I pull into the short-term parking lot and help Vera with her luggage. She came with so little and somehow was leaving the same. Of course she looks beautiful—she looks like her true self. A soft but fitted dress, a cropped cardigan, sandals, and a sunhat she picked up in Biarritz, fit for Bridget Bardot. She is wearing large, cateye sunglasses that make her seem older and hide her reddened eyes.

She hasn't stopped crying since Claudia left. It's not always a full-on bawl, but it's a stream of constant sadness. Each time I see a tear escape beneath her glasses, some other part of me dies inside.

Somehow I manage to soldier on though, and after we've checked her bags and lingered in a café, it's time for her to go through security. It's at this moment when I take back everything I've ever thought about being in love and being a hero.

I feel like a coward.

I feel like a real man would grab hold of her and stop her somehow. Escape from the country with his love by his side.

It would be heavenly to do that, to just run away with her and never look back.

But this man, this tired old sap, has the same re-sponsibilities that most men do. I could never leave my daughter. And my daughter could never leave her mother. And her mother could, *would*, never leave Spain, or even Madrid.

Once again I am tied, that same fucking noose connecting my neck to everyone else's. Would a hero or a coward cut that rope loose?

I don't know. I only know myself.

And now I have to say goodbye to the most real thing I've ever experienced, the true love of my life.

I can't even tell her the words.

Goodbye.

Neither can she.

We stare at each other outside the security line, and every time I want to open my mouth to speak, the words fail me, along with everything else deep inside. All I can do is grab hold of her delicate wrists, feel the silk of her white, inked skin, and look at her intently enough so she can read everything I'm feeling.

I wrap her into my arms and she cries once again. I'd be lying if I said I wasn't crying too. There is only so much a man can take, and this is my limit. You take away Vera, you take away my life. I will feel loss. I will weep.

We stand like that in the airport, her purse and carry-on at her feet, and we ignore the masses of people who pass us on each side. For this one moment, it is just us again in our very real, very small world.

But even our world isn't immune to time.

"I have to go," she says, lightly breathless. She pulls away from me, severing the connection, and I immediately want to scream, to yell, to tell her that this is wrong, that I can't breathe without her, and that she can't go.

It cannot be this way.

And yet it is.

She gives me a half-hearted wave, tears rolling down her face, and heads toward security.

I don't move. I stay there. She looks behind at me once or twice, and we she sees me, she looks surprised, as if she never expected me to wait.

But I do wait.

I wait.

And I wait.

And I wait.

Until she is through security and out the other end. She tosses me a sad, cornered glance over her shoulder, and already I feel like what we are is beginning to split in two. If she changed her mind, she could get to me.

I can't get to her.

I watch her until she disappears out of sight. Then I watch the space where she was for a long time after that. Just me, standing in the airport as everyone else passes by me in a blur.

Just a man in love. Just a hero. Just a coward.

Just me.

I am thirty-nine years old. I was a national football hero. I have a young daughter. An ex-wife.

I lived with the woman of my dreams.

I asked her to marry me.

Now she is gone.

And I am nothing but a black hole.

Time does a peculiar thing when you're grieving. It runs slow, like syrup without the sweetness. For two weeks after Vera left, I barely remember even getting out of bed. The sun and moon rotated, the heat of late summer was replaced by an early autumn chill. I went to work—it was the only time I interacted with people. Every other moment I was by myself, nursing the hollowness that was growing inside me with glass upon glass of old scotch.

I try to have some sort of contact with Vera as much as I can. If I am not texting her, I am talking to her on the phone; if I am not hearing it that way, I am watching her grainy but still beautiful face over Skype. I send pictures to her and she sends pictures to me. My fingers trail down the screen as if I can feel her.

But we are both wounded, fighting our own battles now, in our own countries, with our own enemies. For me, my enemy is still fate. Isabel has let me take Chloe Ann on Wednesdays and weekends again, and the gossip has mercifully stopped. In the last week, I have not had my picture taken by a single photographer, and Carlos Cruz has agreed to take the settlement and the clause that he never post an article or picture about me again.

But the damage is done. I am here and she is there, and we are both suffering. I can read it in every one of her words, hear it in her voice, see it in the shadowy captures of her face. She is miserable and struggling through each day, just as I am. But sometimes, Vera seems more lost than I, and less determined to find her way back.

She is back in her mother's house, in her old room. She says her mother isn't being as bad as she feared but she's certainly not welcoming. I guess at one point Vera was used to the distance and indifference, but now, perhaps after being in Spain with me, with my family, she's learned what warmth feels like. I can attest, just from the few times I've met her, that Vera's mother is as cold as ice, and I can't imagine her thriving in that kind of environment anymore.

Josh, her brother, has been her savior like he has before, but even he can only do so much. Vera tells me that when she's not hanging out with him, she's not doing much of anything. He works at a restaurant and she has nothing to occupy her time. She's not even sure if she's going to get a job or not because every time she applies, it seems her mother brings up future plans. It sounds like she wants Vera to go live in Alberta if she can't commit to Vancouver one hundred percent.

And Vera can't. I am grateful for that, that she's not throwing down roots where her roots used to be. She doesn't want to apply for school in January because she thinks perhaps she can come back to me. Each time I talk to her, I tell her that her future is here, that if we can hold on through these months apart like we once did, we can be together again.

She never sounds very convinced. I feel like our connection is already starting to deteriorate, and I don't know what I can do to fix it. I just try and talk to her as often as I can, tell her I love her as often as I can, and hold a lot of hope in my heart.

But the days are getting colder. Shorter. And yet it does nothing to make the time go faster, to get her in my arms sooner.

It's a miserable day at work. The sky is swollen with dark clouds, and they flood the streets with rain. Even though it's technically still summer, the sudden damp chills me to the bone. It seems everyone is feeling it.

Our main goaltender was injured two weeks after our first official game, and the back-up is having some conflict with Diego. Warren and I watch from the sidelines and you can see the tension rising among the players. There has been too much change for them lately, and it's starting to show. They lost the first game which definitely didn't help the season get off on the right foot and the fair-weather fans have already started to jump off the bandwagon, as they often do.

I am almost done with some paperwork on one of the players when Warren stops by my desk. I glance up at him, about to tell him I'll see him tomorrow, but he just hangs around my work area.

"We need to get a drink," he says to me, folding his arms and leaning against my desk.

"Right now?" I ask, surprised. We've never done anything outside of work together. I haven't even seen Pedro or Antonio outside of work either, not since I started. Seems once you're theirs, the wooing stops.

"It's been a shit day," he says. "Perfect excuse to have a drink, don't you say?"

I shrug but find myself agreeing—every day has been a shit day since Vera left. I grab my jacket and follow him out the door. It's four o'clock, which is a bit early, but it's also the hour of the day that I find myself growing lighter, happier. It's the time that means Vera will be getting up soon. The time difference between us is a terrible burden, and it's hard having to go the majority of my work day without being able to talk to her.

Warren usually takes the metro to work, so we take my SUV and find a bar halfway between his apartment and mine. It's a bit down at its heels and I immediately feel a rock of sadness in my chest, knowing that it's the kind of place that Vera would like.

I miss her so fucking much it hurts.

We sit down and Warren goes to get us a drink. I'm surprised when he comes back with bourbon instead of beer.

"Had a hard day?" I ask him.

He only grins. "Nah, mate, *you've* had a hard day." He clinks his glass against mine. "A hard few weeks, I would think."

I nod slowly, watching him as we tip the liquid into our mouths. When he first asked me for a drink, I had wondered if he wanted to talk about him leaving and me taking over his position, but now I am not so sure.

"How are you holding up?" he asks me. He's curious, but there is no malice in his voice, just true concern.

I take in a long breath. I haven't talked about this—Vera and I—with anyone. When Lucia or my parents breach the subject, I have to walk away. Their voices and faces hold so much emotional attachment to her that it breaks my heart all over again and reminds me what I am missing. Their loss only adds to mine.

But Warren is a somewhat impartial outside party. He has no emotional attachment to her, or to me. He won't even be around for much longer. And because of this, somehow I feel it is safe to tell him the truth, even though it pains me to admit it.

I look down at my glass, swirling the amber liquid around. "I am not holding up," I tell him. "And that is the truth."

His eyes turn sympathetic though not pitying. "I know how that is."

I down the rest of the bourbon, relishing the burn. "I thought I did," I say, clearing my throat. "I thought that because we went through this before I would be able to handle it again. But the person I was back then, the person she was . . . we have both changed so much since then. We have grown. With each other. Into each other, if that makes sense. Before it was tough . . . but this, this is killing me."

It's not like me to ever admit that with someone I don't know but it feels good—freeing—to say it. Hearing it come from my own mouth makes me realize how much it is true. How badly I am being affected. Vera is every-where, every moment of the day, every crevice of my mind, and yet I cannot build her out of my memories, I cannot conjure up her taste, her smell, her skin, her smile, and make a real flesh and blood version of her. She is a prisoner of my mind and heart and soul, and it's not enough for me. I want her real, I want her here. Now. Today. Tomorrow.

Warren sighs, and from the sound of it, I know he understands. He's remembering what it was like for him, how being *this* in love can warp your whole life. But he can't know this pain, he can't know what it's like to lose Vera because he never had Vera. If he had, then he would really know how I'm *handling* things. With scotch. With numbness. With a bleeding heart.

"And so what are you going to do about it?" he asks me, giving me a pointed look.

I shrug. "Wait, I guess. I don't have a choice. She can only get into school in January, *if* she can get in."

"What if she doesn't get in?"

I give him a wry look. "She will. I have ways."

"You have money," he says matter-of-factly.

225

I tilt my hand up and down. "More or less. Money. Influence. Sometimes those things work in my favor. Sometimes they don't."

"So, if you're so sure she's going to get into the school in January, why are you waiting?"

I frown, not sure what he's saying. He raises his hand to get the bartender to bring over two more of the same drink, and I ask him, "What do you mean?"

He gets the same expression on his face as he does when one of our players trips over someone on the field. "I mean, if I were you, and lord knows I'm not, and I had this money and influence and star power and large balls and whatever you have, *and* I could get my girlfriend into a university just because, I wouldn't make her wait until January. I would get her in the university right now. Like, next week if I bloody could."

"The semester has already started," I protest. "There are transcripts that need to come in on time."

He briefly rolls his eyes. "Yes. Your point? Bribe your way in, Mateo. You were prepared to do that anyway. Who cares if the transcripts aren't in, enroll her in something, anything. Start fresh."

And suddenly there is a light bulb going off, but it's not in my mind, it's in my chest, and it's growing brighter, warmer, illuminating everything.

"She would have to fill in the application from Canada," I say. "What if I . . . what if she . . ." What I'm afraid to say is, what if she won't come? What if she has too many excuses? What if it's already too late?

The bartender plunks down the glasses in front of us and Warren lifts his in a salute at me. "You know how it is. If you want something done right, you have to do it yourself. You've got only a short amount of time before you become assistant coach and then another short amount before you are coach. This is the last freedom you'll have—I should know. Maybe you should take advantage of that."

Maybe I should go to her, is what he is saying. Maybe I should go to Vancouver and make sure this happens.

Maybe I should go and bring Vera back home.

I raise my glass and clink it against his, but my mind is already elsewhere. It's already calculating fees and plane tickets and how I'm going to ask the university and how I'm going to ask Pedro for time off. It's thinking about Vera and showing up at her door and touching her, kissing her, holding her.

It's thinking about how having her in front of me will put my worried heart to rest, and that everything will feel whole again. That the world will become balanced once more and the time waiting for the student visa won't feel like time at all because we'll be together.

When I say goodbye to Warren, my heart is already in another time zone. I rush back to the apartment to start getting everything in order.

I won't even tell Vera what's going on until she's in my arms again.

And I will recreate our destiny.

Chapter Twelve

I'm normally a good flier but I have never been so nervous on a plane before. This is far more nerve-wracking than going on the plane to stop Vera. The man sitting next to me in business class keeps asking me if I'm all right. It's kind of him but I don't dare get into specifics, so I just tell him I have a fear of flying.

To distract myself, I bring out the wrinkled letter from my wallet. I read it again and again. I no longer need any reminders of what I'm fighting for because I'm heading straight to her, and I am fighting with all I have. But it still brings me a sense of peace and calm. It's familiar and soothing and it brings me back to all those nights that I spent reading it, wondering about the future.

Now I know the future. It won't be by chance, it will be by choice. If—*when*—I bring Vera back to Spain, it will be another lease on life for us. The same problems we face may still be there, waiting in the bushes. Perhaps not in the form of Carlos Cruz, but in other ways. But at least I know she cannot be taken from me. I can face anything as long as she is by my side.

When the flight lands in Vancouver, I bring out my phone and her mother's address, and step into the blazing hot sunshine. It's almost as if Madrid and Vancouver have traded Septembers. It seems more fitting this way, that the heat and sun follows Vera just as I do.

As I wait in the line for the taxis, I send her a text. It's noon here, which isn't an unusual time for her to hear from me.

What are you doing? I text.

I'm in a cab by the time she replies: *Mercy and dickhead are over for lunch so I'm hiding in my room. How are you baby? I had a dream last night about you, it made me so sad this morning when I realized it was only a dream.*

I can't help the grin that spreads across my face. It does feel like a dream, as if it won't happen, but I am on her soil, in her time, under her sun and sky.

Sometimes dreams come true, I text her back, biting my lip as I do so.

I know they do. I wouldn't have met you if they didn't.

My heart flutters at that and I take in a deep breath. Now my nerves are perking up, creating a knot in my stomach. It's a good knot, holding excitement and promise.

If you could see the stars from where you are, I text her, *would you make a wish on a shooting one? What would you wish for?*

There is a pause before she answers: *You. I watch the stars every night and I wish for you over and over again.*

You have me.

I know. But I don't have you here. Nothing is the same without you.

So your wish, more than anything, would be for me to show up at your doorstep and sweep you off your feet all over again??

I'm already swept off my feet. You did that the day I met you and I haven't come down yet.

Vera doesn't always text with so much emotion, so to read this from her makes me ache. I can't imagine how I would feel if I was reading this, alone in Madrid, knowing how much longer I would have to wait.

Her mother's house isn't too far from the airport and the traffic at this time is kinder than Madrid's. It's not long before the cab is pulling up to the curb.

I tell the driver to keep going a few houses down, just in case there is someone nosy watching at the window. The trees here that line the street are still green, with only a tinge of rust in some of them, signaling the fall. I take off my jacket, feeling the warmth, and then freeze in my shoes when I spot someone coming up the street toward me.

It's Josh, hands in his pockets, head down and listening to music. He's wearing all black—black boots, black jeans, a black denim jacket, and he stands out like a dark mark on the green street. He only looks up just before he heads down the path to the house, and when he does, he does a double take and stops dead in his tracks.

He lifts the headphones off his ears and stares at me in disbelief. "Mateo?" he asks incredulously.

I offer him a wave of my hand and an easy smile. "Hola, Josh."

I walk over to him and he's still staring at me with wide eyes.

"I, uh," he says, his eyes darting to the house and back, "Vera never told me you were coming."

I shrug. "Vera doesn't know."

Now Josh is smiling. "Dude," he says, "you are going to make her fucking year. Hey, good to see you, man."

He puts his hand out for me to shake. I take it but pull him into a quick embrace. He's a little bit taller than me, but Vera herself is pretty tall for a woman. Good genes.

When we pull apart he doesn't seem too uncomfortable with the affection. I forget that men in North America can be a bit funny about physical greetings, and he's a man who I thought, and still hope, will be my brother-in-law one day.

"Good to see you too," I tell him, and I mean it. I give the house an anxious glance. "I just texted her before. Your sister and brother-in-law are home, yes?"

Josh grimaces. "Ugh, probably. I just got off my shift at work." He gives me a reassuring smile and pats me on the shoulder. "Don't worry, I've got your back."

I know he does but I'm worrying anyway.

"Well, come on, let's go put a smile on my sister's face." He gestures for me to follow, and I do so up the stone path to the front door of the elegant house. He tries the door and it opens, and we step inside.

Voices drift down the stairs, coming from the kitchen. I recognize her mother's, her sister's, and the stupid English fellow. Vera really must be hiding out in her room.

I swallow down the pit of nervousness. I'm a fucking grown man for Christ's sake, I shouldn't be scared of her family, but there is that twinge of apprehension as I prepare to face off against people who don't care for me, maybe even despise me. You'd think after everything that has happened to me so far, I would be used to it.

We walk up the stairs, and as soon as we are in the kitchen, three flabbergasted heads swirl toward me.

"Look who I found outside," Josh says in a low voice.

Vera's mother is the first to shut her gaping mouth. Her chin juts out and she squints at me through her glasses. She'd be a beautiful woman if she didn't look so unhappy all the time. "Oh," she says.

Mercy is still aghast, thin brows raised. She doesn't look much like Vera—too thin, too tanned, dressed in skinny jeans and a thin white sweater. She's not bad looking by any means but with her too-sleek hair and face full of makeup she reminds me too much of Isabel.

Then there is her new husband, Charles. He's really too bland to describe. He reminds me of a blanched almond with glasses.

But my manners should never desert me.

I nod at Mercy and Charles and say with as much sincerity as I can muster, "Congratulations on your wedding. I saw the photos and it looked absolutely beautiful. I know Vera and I wish you both a happy marriage."

He is the first to snap out of it. He looks surprised and gives me a nod. "Oh, well thank you."

"Yes," Mercy says, but her tone is cautioning. "I'm sure you must know a lot about marriage."

"Mercy," Josh says sharply, but she merely looks at her mother, I suppose to see what kind of remark she's going to throw in there. I can't say I'm hurt or shocked by this.

"We weren't expecting you," her mother says quickly, and to her credit she shoots Mercy a glare. When she looks back at me, she gives me an uneasy smile. "Vera never said anything about it. Not that she ever tells us anything."

And why should she? I think.

"Vera doesn't know I'm here."

"Oh?" she says, sounding interested now. She adjusts her glasses. "A surprise visit?"

"More or less," I tell her. And suddenly I'm impatient to see Vera. I give them all a nod. "If you'll excuse me though, I should go to her."

I turn, giving Josh an appreciative look, and then head down the hallway toward her bedroom. But it's not her bedroom, and this isn't her house, and she's not at home. She's just in transition, even if she doesn't know it yet.

Outside her door I pause, and I can feel her energy coming through the wood. It makes my hairs stand on end, puts flames to every part of my body. I am so close I can't even stand it.

I take in a deep breath and then knock.

There is silence, then a shuffling sound, and a grumpy cry of, "What? I'm taking a nap."

I smile to myself at that and then slowly open the door.

She's in her bed and under the covers, her wild hair spilling over the pillow. Her eyes are closed and the minute that I shut the door behind me, they snap open.

"Actually, it's called a siesta," I tell her.

She sits up and blinks at me for a few moments, looking both girlish and sexual. "Am I dreaming?" And then she seems to actually believe she is because she pinches the tattoo on her forearm.

"Pinching won't do," I say, and before my heart can explode, I cross the room and lean over her bed, kissing her long, deep, and soft on the lips. I hear her gasp under my lips and tongue and feel her tremble as my hands coast into the satin waves of her hair.

I'm enveloped by everything she offers—her taste, her smell, her touch, her feel. I could die a very happy man right now. My own heart thumps rapidly, loudly, out of control, as if even it can't deal with the fact that I have my love in my arms again.

"Mateo," she whimpers against me, and then I taste the salt of her tears as they roll toward our hungry, deprived mouths.

I can't get any closer to her, can't hold on to her any tighter, and yet she feels just like I've dreamed. Real. Whole. Loved. I feel like I'm dying and being reborn at the same time.

"My Estrella," I manage to murmur as I start to kiss every square inch of her face. "I've come to take you home."

"How are you here?" she says, her nails digging into the back of my shirt. "How is this possible?"

"I am here because you are mine," I tell her, kissing her behind the ear and breathing in deeply. "And I am yours. I belong with you, and you belong with me. I don't care which country or where or under what stars but without you, I'm only me."

"Oh, Mateo" she says softly, her voice choked. She cups the back of my head with a delicate hand and holds me close to her. "I'm so glad you came. I don't think I could have survived another day. Being apart from you . . . it's been destroying me more than I've let you know. I . . . I'm in so much pain all the time."

"Shhh," I gently reassure her, my fingers trailing down her back. "You don't have to be in pain anymore. I am here. I am not leaving without you by my side."

She swallows loudly and buries her head into the crook of my neck. Her lips tickle my collarbone as she speaks, and it sends a wave of pleasure down my chest. "But how can we do this? I still can't go back to Spain yet and you can't be without Chloe Ann."

"That is what I thought too," I admit, kissing the rim of her earlobe. She shivers. "But then I realized I wasn't looking hard enough. Are you ready to hear the plan? Because we can be together, from this moment forward. It just depends on you."

She pulls away and stares at me deeply with red-rimmed eyes. "I'll do whatever," she whispers, and cups my face with her hands. "You know I'll do whatever."

I didn't know that, but now I do. I close my eyes and breathe a sigh of relief, feeling foolish for even doubting her to begin with. Distance does funny things to truth, twists it and paints one side with doubt.

I brush her hair from her face and kiss her gently. "That is good to hear. You don't understand how much I've worried about you, that . . . perhaps you've learned to love me less while you've been here."

Her eyes widen in shock. "What? How could you think that? Mateo, I've been dying without you."

I smile gently. "That shouldn't make me happy but it does. Especially because you don't have to die anymore. Vera, I've contacted the University of Madrid. They will take you in as a student—now—and you can start the semester just a little late. You're smart. You can catch up."

She stares at me, brows knitting together. "How is that possible?"

"Let's just say that I have my ways."

"You bribed them?"

I hope she doesn't get funny over this. I exhale quietly. "Yes. In one way or another."

Although in reality it is a lot more straightforward than that. I wrote a check for her tuition for the first year, and then I added an extra ten thousand dollars to that check. A nice little donation for whatever department needs it the most. Under budget lately, they gladly took it.

"Oh," she says softly.

I grab her hands, shaking them slightly. "This was the only way, and it is a good way. It is all in place. You will take Spanish as your main degree. It isn't astronomy, but they said something about online classes used in the future, and there are hospitality and tourism classes offered in English, very popular with people from the UK. I know it's not ideal but once your university here in BC pushes through with your transcript, they seem to think you can still walk out with a bachelor's degree. It just might take longer than usual. But more than that, the visa will let you live in the country for another few years, and that's all that really matters at this point."

"What happens after that?" she asks warily.

I squeeze her hands. "We will be together, somehow, some way. Perhaps you can get a job through my work or we can apply for common law after a while. With the time this allows us, we can work something out together." I swallow the lump forming in my throat. "Please tell me you'll do this."

She slumps slightly. "Of course I will. It's just a lot to take in . . ."

"You knew I was going to pay for the tuition anyway."

"I know," she says, looking down at our entwined hands. "I just feel bad that you have to take care of me."

"Vera," I tell her, "I don't have to take care of you. You can take care of yourself. I *want* to take care of you. Please let me."

She nods quickly, and a tear slides down her cheek. "Okay." She looks up at me and her smile is brighter than the sun. I immediately feel warmer. "Okay. Thank you."

Yet I should be thanking her. I pull her to me and hold her tight, feeling the happiness radiate from within me, within her. We stay like that for a few moments, just feeling heartbeats, skin, and breath.

"So what do I need to do?" she asks me.

I slowly get to my feet and stand above her, stretching my arms and getting the ten-hour flight out of my system. I'm suddenly exhausted.

"I have the forms with me," I say, gesturing to my carry-on I left behind her door. "You'll fill them in just as if you were a first year student. They already have the tuition. I'll courier it to them and then we take your acceptance letter to the Spanish consulate here and get your visa rolling."

"How long is it going to take?" she asks.

I shrug. "They assured me it wouldn't be long. Maybe a few weeks."

"So when are you going back?"

I grin down at her. "Estrella, I am not going back without you."

"But Chloe Ann, your job . . . you just started."

"It's all right," I tell her reassuringly. "I spoke with Pedro, Diego, Warren . . . this is the best time for me to go. In the future, I won't have so much time. And my daughter is fine, we will see her as usual when we get back. Let's just have a vacation while we wait."

"But what if the paparazzi start up again when I return?" she asks. "What if that spurs Isabel and her family into another tirade against us?"

I sigh, my heart still heavy over that. "We can only just survive it. Hold our heads high. It's not going to be easy, and I still don't think it's going to go away completely. But at least the settlement has prevented Cruz from saying anything, and with you in the country legally, there is nothing anyone can do to us. It will hurt and sting at times when they throw around the lies, but we are strong enough to withstand it now." I kiss her hand and stare at her deeply. "I think we will always pay for our sins, Vera, but our sins have been worth it. Haven't they?"

She nods. "I'd walk through coals for you."

"You already have," I say. "And I wish you didn't have to. But it is what it is."

"And it's beautiful," she says. Then she gets out of bed and wraps her arms around me.

It *is* beautiful.

I end up spending three weeks in Vancouver. The process for the student visa takes a bit longer than expected. It's a pity you can't bribe the government the way you can other institutions, but Vera and I manage to make the most of it.

The day I arrived at her mother's house in Vancouver, we ended up having dinner with her family. It wasn't exactly a comfortable, smooth experience, and her sister grated on my nerves so badly that it took a lot to keep my temper in check. But by the end of it, it seemed that that they were warming up to me. At least Vera's mother was able to put away her prejudices. Perhaps it helped that I had come all the way for Vera and was actively trying to get her to return to Spain. It should have at least proved that I was serious about her.

After that, however, we were out of there. When the paperwork was all filed and couriered, we rented a car and went on a road trip to the center of the province, a place called the Okanagan. It reminded me a lot of Spain—dry rolling hills the color of khaki and wheat, cold blue lakes, orchards and vineyards as far as the eye could see. It felt less like waiting and more like truly relaxing, enjoying the hot, prolonged summer.

There was a lot of lazing around, a lot of wine, a lot of love-making. Being inside Vera again was like coming home, and her skin, her lips, her touch, was the map that led me there. It was exactly what we needed to reconnect again, and I think when we emerged from our bliss, we somehow came out stronger.

When we finally are granted her visa, there is a surprisingly emotional goodbye between her and her family. Though Josh seems sad to see her go, he's also happy because she's happy. But it's her mother again that surprises me. It makes me think that over time, perhaps she and Vera can have a better relationship. As I said before, distance can do funny things, and sometimes space brings people closer.

On the long plane ride to Madrid, during the night when the cabin lights are off and most of the passengers, including Vera, are asleep, I take out my letter. I read it over, once again out of habit. When I turn my head to look at Vera, I am surprised to see her looking at me with wondering eyes.

"What do you keep reading?" she asks me quietly.

I give her a small smile. "It's probably silly, but it comforts me." I pause and place my hand over hers. "When you left me last year, before I decided I had to come after you, I wrote you a letter. It was an apology for everything I had done."

Her face crumples softly. "Why didn't you give it to me?"

"Because I felt my apologies would be better in person. Was I wrong?"

She shakes her head. "No. No, you didn't even need to apologize to begin with."

I hold it out for her. "Would you like to read it?"

She stares at the paper. "If it's another glimpse at your heart . . . I would love to."

I open her hand and place it inside. "Be gentle with it."

She gingerly takes it, flips on the light above her head, and reads it over in silence. It seems fitting that she's reading it beside me on a plane that is taking us home.

I shouldn't, but I can't help but watch her face. It's so intimate, knowing she's taking in my truth right in front of me. Her eyes well up and she places one hand at her heart, but she doesn't cry. She reads the whole thing in one go. When she is done, she only says, "I love you." But she says so much more than the simplicity of her words. She says everything I have needed to hear.

"I love you," I tell her, and she lays her head on my shoulder. I kiss the top of her head and turn off the lights above us.

Chapter Thirteen

Six months later

"At some point, are you going to tell me where we are going?" Vera says from beside me.

I glance at her over my sunglasses. "Wow, look at you all bossy."

She sticks her tongue out at me. "I'm always bossy. You love it."

I shrug. "This is true. Especially in the bedroom."

She rolls her eyes but a small smile teases her lips. Both of us know that I'm usually the boss in that area.

It is the end of April and Vera only just finished her last exam for the university this past week. I thought a great way to celebrate would be to take her on a short trip for the weekend. Next month, she's going to be working part-time at a hotel as a front desk clerk, part of her hospitality internship she is doing through school, and I will be busy getting my players ready for another season in the football league.

The last six months haven't been easy, but they have been worth it. This time around, Vera has had an easier go of things and for that I am grateful. She caught up in her courses at school fairly quickly and I was surprised by her work and study ethic. Her partying with Claudia was cut down to a minimum and when she wasn't with me, she was studying hard for both her classes and her Spanish.

As for me, being the coach has been one of my greatest challenges. While I think I learned a lot from Diego and Warren before they left, it didn't prepare me for the way the team dynamics change once you're in the position and how different guiding these men is once you're the one leading the way. When games are lost I feel it is my fault, and I am sure I am about to be fired. When we win games, I don't feel like my coaching had anything to do with it. On rough days, I wonder if I am the man for this job and if someone else could handle it better.

But I soldier on. I ignore the backlash *and* the praise. I can only do my best and push myself to do better. Vera and I have, once again, become darlings of the paparazzi, but as the months roll past, the focus becomes more on me and my coaching and less on her and our relationship. It's been about six weeks now since the last picture of us was printed in the tabloids.

That has helped Isabel, too. After the slander her family spread about me, I was expecting to hear more from them, but they also tapered off. I don't know if Isabel got them to do the right thing or if they just stopped trying once they realized that nothing would keep Vera and me apart. Isabel has started seeing a well-known TV personality, so that has probably helped too. She's certainly more pliable when it comes to my visits with Chloe Ann.

The more that Vera improves her Spanish and gains confidence from her studies, the more her bond with Chloe Ann grows. They get along very well, and Vera has started to tell her bedtime stories which makes my heart flip.

There is so much more though that I want. I still want Vera to be my wife and the mother of my children. I've made sure not to push her or even bring it up again for fear of scaring her. But it wasn't until she gave me something of hers that gave me the courage to try again.

When we first got back to the apartment after being in Vancouver, there was a surplus of mail piled up. One of them was a letter from Vera. She had written to me while she was gone and mailed it only a few days before I arrived to get her.

When I found the letter, I asked if I could read it since Vera had read mine. She told me I could but only when I really needed to. I wasn't sure what that meant, so I put her letter away and didn't think twice about it.

Then, one particularly cold March evening, when she was at her Spanish class and I was at home, I felt a pinch of worry in my heart, that feeling that still after everything, she would never truly be mine. Instead of reaching for my own letter, as I usually would, I reached for hers.

Her letter was short, but it was everything I needed. She said she had written it in the middle of the night when she couldn't sleep and her heart was filled with knives. She told me she loved me, that she couldn't stand to be apart from me, and that she was sorry about the way she had turned down my proposal. She said that looking back, she knew I had been genuine and wished that she had not been so swept away by her own fears and panic about the future to realize that she should have said yes.

She wanted to say yes. Yes to marriage, yes to children, yes to everything.

That letter saved me that night and every night after that. Her beautiful, simple, sweet words nestled their way deep inside my soul and continued to bloom there.

"This looks familiar," Vera says, and brings my attention back to her. She peers at a sign on the side of the highway that tells you how many kilometers to Salamanca. "I've been here before."

She has but I don't say anything.

Still, when another hour goes past, she starts fidgeting in her seat, her eyes bright and wide.

"Oh my god," she says. "I know where you are taking me."

"That took you long enough," I tell her with a smile.

"Better late than never," she says. "Acantilado!" Then her eyes seem to darken, her face falling slightly. "Are we going to Las Palabras?"

I shake my head. "We are staying at the same hotel we were at for the program, but they are not holding it there this year. We won't have to see any of those jerks who let you go, don't worry about it. It's just you and me."

"Two years later," she says.

"Two years later."

Soon I am pulling the car up the hill toward the reception and the cabins, and a million memories are smacking me right in the face. I am remembering us walking off the bus, the nervous glances I kept shooting her, the way she was making my body feel alive for the first time, the danger she represented. Now, as I stare at her sitting beside me in the passenger seat, she is no longer dangerous and I am no longer nervous, but she still makes me feel more alive than I'll ever feel.

"Shall we check in?" I ask her, my heart fluttering slightly. All right, perhaps I am just a little nervous after all.

She nods, looking bewildered, maybe by the same memories that are accosting me. We make our way to the front desk, which is run by someone different than last time. They are very welcoming and nice, and though everything looks the same, the hotel has families and couples staying there and that gives it all a very different vibe.

It's familiar but changed, just like us.

We put our bags away in our room and I fight the urge to throw Vera on the bed and have my way with her. It would definitely help with my mounting nerves but there is something else that must happen first.

"Would you like to go for a walk?" I ask her after she's freshened up. I hold my arm out for her and she takes it with a jaunty smile.

"Why, that would be lovely," she says. She looks absolutely radiant which only makes my heart speed up by a few beats.

We walk arm in arm outside the hotel. The spring air is warm but fresh, bringing in the fragrant smell of flowers from the fields. I breathe in deeply, filling my lungs with clarity and strength, and bring her down the hill to the road.

"Are we going where I think we are going?" she asks me, her eyes twinkling.

I only rub the small of her back and lead her off the road and toward the field. There, behind the fence, is a wide stretch of golden grass against blue sky, and in the middle of it all the tree where we first made love.

We walk through the grass, hand in hand, my grip on hers becoming tighter as my breath becomes shorter.

Butterflies rise from the field and scatter in the air around us, and I feel like nature is conspiring with me.

We stand beneath the tree. The green canopy of leaves stretches out over our heads like an umbrella, and the area at our feet is as wild and overgrown as before. All around us is that wonderfully blue sky and the rolling golden hills dotted with old stone houses and square plots of farm. Birds call to each other from the grass, cicadas click in the distance.

I turn so that I'm facing Vera, staring down at her, and I feel like I'm about to pass out. She's so beautiful and good, I can't possibly deserve her. But if I have the chance to make her mine forever, I am going to take it.

Again.

I clear my throat and put my hand at her cheek, looking at her intently. "Vera," I say. "Two years ago I saw you on the bus . . . and you changed my whole life. Two years ago your gorgeous smile, your wonderful spirit, your raw, beautiful soul, took me on a journey that I never thought I'd go on. You shook me up, over and over again, until I didn't know what way was up, but I knew the way out was you. Out of the cold, black and white, empty world I was living in and into yours—

ours—one of heat and color. You've opened my eyes and my heart. You've made me a better man, a better person. You've made me realize that while sometimes love can't conquer all, it can conquer you. You've conquered me, Vera, and I am forever yours." I take in a shaky breath, squeeze her hand, and drop to one knee. "Will you be forever mine?"

Her eyes widen then blink rapidly as I take out a small velvet box from my jacket pocket. With my hand slightly trembling, I flip it open to reveal the silver amethyst and diamond ring that Lucia helped me pick out a few weeks ago. It's sparkling, shining, rare and precious just like Vera.

"Vera, will you marry me?" I ask, and hold my breath because if she says no, I am not sure I want to breathe again.

She seems stunned, speechless for a few moments, and I fear I might die. But then she nods quickly, and her eyes water, and she breaks out into a smile so beautiful it takes my breath away anyway.

"Si," she says, and then giggles. "Yes, yes, yes, yes, yes!"

My heart is bursting as I fumble for the ring and manage to slip it on her finger. We both admire it on her slender hand for a moment—it looks like it was meant for her—before I pull her down to the grass beside me.

I grab her face in my hands and let out a cry of delight. I kiss her mouth, her nose, her cheek, her forehead, and pull her into me, wrapping my arms around her. I am laughing; I am joy and so is she.

"You are going to be my wife," I tell her, nuzzling her neck.

"You will be my husband," she says, laughing too. "Oh, I was so afraid I had lost my chance, that you would never ask me again."

I pull back and kiss a tear that has rolled down her cheek. "I would never stop asking," I tell her. "We belong with each other. I would never stop until it was made right."

"It is more than right now," she says. "It's fucking everything. I'm going to be Mrs. Mateo Casalles." Her face turns down for a moment. "I hope I can make you proud."

"You will always make me proud, just by being you," I tell her, kissing her long and deep on the lips, feeling the urge to physically make her mine as well. "And if you want to be a wife who makes drunken lemonade while wearing sexy little dresses, that will make me proud too."

She grins. "You wouldn't even be able to stop me."

"I don't ever want to stop you," I say, and gently lower her back so that she's lying in the grass. "Wherever you go, I follow."

And now, I will follow her to the very end.

I quickly look around to make sure no lone farmer is wandering nearby and remove my pants.

Vera lies in the grass, grinning saucily, and hikes her dress up around her waist. She's not wearing underwear. Neither am I. Match made in heaven.

I pin her arms above her head, her hair pooling around her, and slowly push myself into her. She's wet and wanting, and I can't believe I'm going to marry her, marry this, this perfect place where I finally feel at home. I fit inside her like I belong there, and she wraps her legs around the small of my back, driving me in, keeping me close to her. We move as one—we are one.

We make love, fast and slow and frantic and controlled. Our bodies take us through every emotion, every feeling, every desire. There in the field, under that tree, beneath the Spanish sun, we have come full circle. When

I pour myself into her, I feel like I'm giving her every essence of me, and as she comes around me, I feel like she's trying to keep me inside her forever.

I stay inside for as long as I can. Then I put my arms around her and she nestles into my chest, and we stare up at the rustling leaves, at the sky and space and stars hidden behind the sun.

I can feel her smile against my skin.

I smile back.

Our love is permanent and she is stardust in my hands.

I could never want for anything more.

THE END

If you have enjoyed this book, please consider leaving a review on Amazon, GoodReads, Barnes & Noble or any other review site. Authors really appreciate it.

Want to say hola? Drop me a line at authorkarinahalle@gmail.com and I'll do my best to get back to you. I love hearing from my readers (when they say nice things, hate mail will not be read). Want to follow me on Instagram? You should. I'm awesome on it. @authorhalle.

TIME FOR THE THANKS

It's hard to thank everyone so I'm going to keep it short and sweet. Scott, Laura, Barbie and Stephanie – thank you for being my sounding boards as I hemmed and hawed over whether I was doing Mateo justice or not. Najla for her wonderful cover and Ellie for helping me secure just the right Mateo. Kara for her concise editing. Scott, again, because you're my number one fan. My editor at Atria, Jhanteigh, and all the peeps there for letting me put Where Sea Meets Sky in here. My agent, Taylor, for being awesome. My PR guru Danielle for going above and beyond. Bruce, because he's the cutest dog in the world. Oh and I should mention that Vera's new tattoo is *not* an original. Jodi M. Bibliophile (Mateo's wife, if you don't know it yet) got it first.

Love in Spanish is ALL OF YOU!!!

Keep reading to read the first chapter of Where Sea Meets Sky (it's about Vera's brother Josh, you don't want to miss it!).

ABOUT THE AUTHOR

With her USA Today bestselling The Artists Trilogy published by Grand Central Publishing, numerous foreign publication deals, and self-publishing success with her Experiment in Terror series, Vancouver-born Karina Halle is a true example of the term "Hybrid Author." Though her books showcase her love of all things dark, sexy and edgy, she's a closet romantic at heart and strives to give her characters a HEA...whenever possible.

Karina holds a screenwriting degree from Vancouver Film School and a Bachelor of Journalism from TRU. Her travel writing, music reviews/interviews and photography have appeared in publications such as Consequence of Sound, Mxdwn and GoNomad Travel Guides. She currently lives on an island on the coast of British Columbia where she's preparing for the zombie apocalypse with her husband and rescue pup.

Make sure you don't miss it! *Read on for a peek at the next new adult novel by Karina Halle.* Available from Atria Books in eBook and trade paperback in March 2015

<u>CHAPTER ONE</u>

<u>Vancouver</u>

Josh

I get an erection the moment I first lay eyes on her. She looks like no one I've ever seen before. Tall, curvy, with thick superhero thighs and a round ass, showcased in black Lycra that hugs every slope. Her big, high breasts and small waist are accentuated by her white tank top. Her body has just enough meat for me to grab a good hold of, and I imagine running my hands over her hills and valleys. I want to imagine more than that, but I'm horny as hell as it is and my erection is already inappropriate, considering I'm in public and all.

She finally looks my way, aware that I've been staring like an idiot. She catches my gaze, her eyes twinkling a vibrant yellow, her pupils large and wet. She smirks at me, causing a shower of glitter to rain from her cheeks, and brushes her purple hair over her shoulder before she bends over to slide a gun out from the harness strapped to her boot.

I try not to stare into the blinding sun of her tanned cleavage. I try to think of something clever to say to her. Something along the lines of, *I think I know who you are, but shouldn't you have one eyeball instead of two?*

But it's she who comes over to me, gun comfortably in her hand, and stops only a foot away. When she smiles at me, I see fangs.

Now I'm really confused. At least I know what to say now.

"Who are you?" I ask her, happy that my voice is hard and deep. I hope it makes her think of sex.

She raises a perfect brow, and up close I'm struck by how bronzed her skin tone is. I don't think it's makeup. Not many people in Vancouver manage to keep their tan into the fall.

"You don't know?" she asks. She has an accent. I immediately want to say she's from England but that's not it. It's not Australia either.

"I thought I did," I say. "But your eyes and fangs are throwing me all off."

"I'm vampire Leela, from *Futurama*."

I grin at her, happy that I was half-right. "Shouldn't you just have *one* eyeball then?"

She reaches into her other boot and effortlessly pulls out an eye mask. It's painted white, with a black pupil in the middle. She waves it at me. "I put it on for photos but I can barely see out of it. I walked into a wall, twice." She raises two fingers for emphasis. "I figured I'll just be a vampire the rest of the time."

I can seriously listen to her talk all day. "I don't remember any episode where Leela turned into a vampire." Maybe it hinted at my secret nerd-boy status, but I watched the cartoon *Futurama* religiously.

She wets her lips for a moment and I try my hardest not to adjust my boxer briefs underneath my costume. "I like to think she'll become a vampire in future episodes. Or maybe she was one once and Matt Groening scrapped the idea. I believe characters have more to their lives than the lives we are shown."

"Kind of like people," I say, hoping I come across as somewhat profound.

She gives me a slight nod – indicating I'm not as profound as I thought – and looks me up and down. "I just had to come over here to tell you you're the best-dressed guy here. I mean, that must have taken some effort."

I grin at her. "*Game of Thrones* fan?" I ask.

Another sly nod. "Of course. But who doesn't love Khal Drogo?"

"Last year I dressed up as George R.R. Martin," I tell her. "People kept mistaking me for Ernest Hemingway, even though I was carrying a bucket of fried chicken around with me and had a pillow stuffed down my shirt."

"So you went for something sexier..." she says as she lets her eyes trail over my body, which automatically makes me stand up straighter. I haven't left much to the imagination. Jesus sandals, weird billowy pants that I think some granola dude dropped off at the thrift store, plus a leather corset over my abs and leather cuffs on my forearms. My upper body is bare and covered with bronzer and streaks of blue paint, and I found a black wig with a long braid down the back. It kind of works. I guess if you don't know the show, I look like some sparkling warrior who wears too much eye makeup.

"Hey, girls can't be the only ones to slut it up at Halloween."

She raises her brow.

And once again, my foot goes in my mouth. "I mean, not that you're dressed slutty or anything, I just mean--"

She laughs. "Don't worry about it," she says with a wave of her hand. "*Everyone* here is dressed slutty. That's what the holiday is about, isn't it? Pretending to be someone else? This is actually my first Halloween, so I'm feeling a little overdressed. Or super nerdy." She looks around her at the drunk girls—referees and fairies and nurses in wonderfully-indecent outfits—and shrugs.

"I wholeheartedly disagree," I say, trying not to ogle her all over again. I pause. "Wait, your first Halloween?"

"First *proper* Halloween. The North American kind. We don't really celebrate it the way you guys do."

I cross my arms, insanely curious now. "And who is we?"

"New Zealand," she says. "I'm from Auckland."

"Nice," I say, "I was going to ask if you were from New Zealand."

Her lips twitch and she gives me a shake of her head. "No you weren't."

"Well, I definitely wasn't going to ask if you were from Australia. I know how you'd feel about that."

For a moment her features look strained, then it passes. "Kind of like if I asked if you were American."

"Exactly."

"So," she muses and steps closer. She lays her hand on my bicep and I suck in my breath. "Are the tattoos real?" She removes her hand and peers at her palm, which is streaked with bronze shimmer shit. "Because your tan sure isn't."

Damn, I hope I'm not blushing. I clear my throat. "The tattoos are real, I assure you. I needed a bit of, um, help to get that Dothraki tan going on."

"And this?" she reaches for my face and am frozen in place while she gently fingers my goatee and beard. She grabs the end of it, which I had attempted to braid, and gives it a little tug.

"Ouch," I say, though it doesn't really hurt. It turns me on instead. Big surprise.

"So it is real," she says. She sounds impressed.

I shrug. "I had a month to grow it in. I say, it's all or nothing. But tomorrow everything is getting shaved off."

She frowns and lets go. "Pity. I love a scruffy guy."

I can't help but smile. "Lucky for you, I'm scruffy for at least twelve more hours."

Her mouth twists into a wry smile. I realize I'm being kind of forward with her, but at the same time she just felt my bicep and fondled my man hair. Then again, I've never been very good at reading women. Half of them seem to love my tats and black hair and piercings; the other half seem to think I'm a delinquent from Skid row.

I'm wondering what she thinks about me when I realize I don't know her name.

"I'm Josh, by the way," I say to her, holding out my hand.

She gives me a surprisingly firm shake in return. "Gemma."

"That's a beautiful name," I tell her. Even though I'm sincere, I'm aware that it's very much a pick-up line.

Gemma snorts and it's absolutely adorable. "Right. Well, in New Zealand, Gemmas are everywhere."

268

"But I bet they don't look like you." Okay, so now I'm totally swerving into pick-up line territory. I push it further. "Can I buy you drink?"

And there the question sits, floating between us along with the haze of pot smoke that hangs in the air. The rejection might come fast, or if I'm lucky, not at all. But it's Halloween, I have a three-beer buzz going on, and I'm feeling pretty good.

Still, when she nods and says, "Sure" I feel my whole body lift with relief.

We make our way through the crowd to the makeshift bar set-up in the corner. It's a house party we're at, one I try and go to every year. My friend Tobias rents the whole house with three other dudes who go to the University of British Columbia nearby, and every Halloween they go all out with mind-fuck decorations, elaborate costumes, and a haunted house in the basement. This year they even applied for a liquor license since last year ended with a police raid and all of us running for our lives down the street.

While we get in line behind a guy dressed as a one-night stand (complete with a lampshade head) and a girl dressed as some Disney princess, I ask her, "So,

Gemma from New Zealand, how did you hear about the party?"

She fixes her yellow eyes on me and I wish she could take out her contacts so I could see their real color. I'm assuming they're brown, based on her skin tone, and I feel like I could get lost in them if she'd let me.

"At the backpackers I'm staying at. I made friends with the guy who works the front desk," she says, and I can't help but feel my entire back bristle. A guy? Of course she'd be here with a guy. "He invited me and another backpacker but I haven't seen them all night." Her eyes sweep the room then come back to me, sparkling knowingly. "Not that I'm surprised; she's from Holland and has legs up to here." She makes a slicing motion with her hand across her neck. "He obviously wanted to shag her."

"Maybe he wanted to shag the both of you," I say and then try not to wince.

She gives me an exasperated look but still smiles. She has the cutest dimples. "Maybe. But I don't like to share. My parents never taught me to play very well with my toys."

"Sup, Drogo," the bartender says. I swivel my head and eye him, slightly annoyed at being interrupted. He's dressed as a hot dog.

"Sup, dog," I say. "Is that costume supposed to be a hint or something?"

He nods, completely deadpan, which only makes it funnier considering there's just a small cut-out for his face in the wall of wiener. "It's a complete metaphorical representation of my penis, if that's what you mean."

Gemma laughs. "You Canadians talk about your dicks a lot."

I casually lean one arm against the bar top. "Well, have you seen our dicks? It's a point of pride for our country."

"No, actually, I haven't," she says and a million clever follow-ups flow through my head. Unfortunately, half of them are serious propositions so I don't dare say them.

"Oh really," the hot dog says, beating me to it. "You know, that can be arranged."

"I'm sure it can," she says sweetly but her eyes are telling him not to bother. "Could I get a beer please? None of that Molson Canadian stuff, though. Do you have any craft brew?"

The hot dog plucks a bottle of Granville Island Winter Ale from the ice chest and plunks it on the counter. "Seven dollars."

I sigh and order one for myself, fishing out my money from a small leather satchel around my waist that I thought maybe Khal Drogo would use when he wasn't slicing people's arms off. "I thought the point of a house party was to have cheap booze."

He shrugs, apparently hearing that complaint all night. "Blame government regulation. Still better than being stuck at some bullshit club downtown."

He has that right.

"Mojo" by Peeping Tom suddenly comes on over the speakers and the rolling beat of one of my favorite songs gives me another boost of confidence. I'm about to suggest to Gemma that we find somewhere to sit, maybe in another room, when she asks if I want to go to the roof deck.

I can't help but oblige.

"It might be still raining," I tell her as we squeeze through the crowd of people and up the carpeted stairs to the second floor. "It's almost winter here, remember."

"Nah, I love the rain," she answers.

"Then you should seriously consider moving here." Suddenly there's a bit of traffic near the door to the roof and she stops in front of me. I'm pressed up against her ass and it's like I've gone to heaven. It's so firm and round that I'm starting to think that she's magic. Of course, I'm also growing harder by the second and I know, *I know*, she can feel the magician's wand.

I cringe inwardly. I really don't want to be one of *those* guys. In fact, I start thinking that perhaps I need to apologize for my public displays of erection but she actually presses her ass back into me. It was subtle but it was there.

Before I drown in over-analysis of the moment, the foot traffic moves forward again and suddenly there is space and we find ourselves up on the flat roof of the building. The air is sharp, cold, and damp, but I have enough alcohol in me that I don't mind the chill. It's stopped raining. There are a few dripping lawn chairs scattered about and scantily-clad girls shivering in their costumes, trying to puff down their cigarettes or joints.

In the distance, you can see the dark mass of English Bay peppered with tankers and the night-skiing lights of Grouse Mountain. The glass high rises of downtown

Vancouver twinkle and set the low clouds an electric shade of orange.

Gemma grabs my hand and leads me to the edge of the roof, away from everyone else. Her grip is strong but her hand warm and soft, and before I can give it a squeeze, she lets go. She leans against the railing, not caring if her arms get cold and wet, and stares out at the view.

"I do have to say, I always thought Auckland one of the most beautiful cities in the world, but Vancouver has totally blown it away," she muses wistfully, her eyes roaming the cityscape.

"How long are you here for?"

She sighs. "Not long enough. Ten days."

"Did you go to Whistler?"

She smiles. "So I could be surrounded by Aussies and other Kiwis? I was there for a day. Nice place. But we have mountains like that back home."

I ask her if she was in other parts of Canada and she tells me she originally got a work permit because she wanted to live and work on Prince Edward Island out east.

I laugh. "Really? Why? You a fan of Anne of Green Gables?"

In the dark, it's hard to tell if she's blushing. "Actually, yes."

"That's cute."

"Shut up." But she's smiling and brushing her hair off her shoulder. "Anyway, work was hard to find there. I guess all the summer jobs were filled, so after a while I had to move on. Went to Nova Scotia, Quebec, Toronto." I scrunch my nose at the last city and she rolls her eyes. "Yeah, yeah, you guys with your rivalry. Then I went down into the States for a few months. Boston, New York. Flew to New Orleans, drove through the Southwest, then onto California. Disneyland." Her eyes light up at that one. "San Francisco. Took a backpacker bus up the Oregon coast, spent some time in Seattle, and now I'm here, flying out tomorrow."

"And you did all of this by yourself?" I ask incredulously.

She purses her lips and nods. "Yeah. Why not?"

"You sound a lot like my sister," I say.

She frowns. "That's not exactly what you want to hear from someone you find attractive."

I stare at her for a few beats, making sure I heard that right. I try not to grin, but I can't help it.

"Attractive?" I repeat.

"Oh, I've gone and given you a big ego, haven't I?"

"Sweetheart, I already had a big ego," I admit, still smiling. "And I don't mean I think you're *just* like my sister, Vera. It's just that she went overseas to Europe last year—Spain, actually—by herself and now she's living there. It's just…" I try and think of the word, "*brave*, that's all. Everyone else I know goes and travels in groups and pairs."

She shrugs. "People can be a pain in the ass."

I nod. "True. But I think it takes some sort of courage to go overseas alone. Don't you get lonely?"

For a moment, I swear she looks lonely. Then it's gone and her expression is blasé. "Not really. I like my own company and I meet heaps of people this way, people I probably wouldn't have met if I were traveling with someone. Sometimes you…wish certain people were around, and sometimes you wish you could share a moment or two with someone else, but fuck, that's what Instagram is for."

I raise my beer at her. "Well, let me just tell you that I think you're a pretty awesome woman, Gemma."

She raises her brow and her bottle at the same time. "Woman? Not chick, not girl?"

"You're all woman to me, as far as I can see," I say.

She clinks her bottle against mine. "It's the tits, isn't it?"

My eyes drift over her. "It's a lot of things." The truth is, I'm torn between wanting to tear her clothes off and fuck her senseless or wanting to sit somewhere quiet and talk to her the whole night. It's a curious war I'm fighting, but I'd be happy with either victory.

"So, you," she says, turning around so she's leaning back on her elbows, one boot kicked up onto the other, "tell me about Josh. All I know is you have a sister called Vera who lives in Spain, you watch *Futurama* and *Game of Thrones*, and you have a big ego and a nice dick."

I choke on my beer and quickly wipe my mouth. "Whoa, whoa, whoa. Who told you about the dick?"

She takes a polite sip of her drink, her eyes playful. "You did earlier. You said it was a Canadian thing."

"Right," I say, quickly recovering. "Well, that's where the ego comes from."

"Uh-huh," she says. "And what do you do? You know, work-wise?"

My smile falters. This part is where I kind of suck at life. A big dick can only get you so far. "Oh, I just kinda work. Jobs."

"Oh, *jobs*," she says. "I've heard of those."

I sigh inwardly. "I'm a line cook at a restaurant."

She cocks her head. "Oh, so you want to be a chef?"

"Not really," I say, but what I mean to say is *not at all.* "It's just something that pays the bills." The minute I say that, it's like I'm lying, because while I do pay rent, I pay it to my mother and it's nowhere near as much as what most people pay. The dirty truth is, I live at home and there's no woman alive who finds that sexy.

"So then what do you like to do, if that's not it?"

Here's the thing. On the surface, Joshua Miles is a charmer. I'm tall, have a good body, nice tats, and a dick that I know how to use. I can be shameless but funny enough, which usually works to my advantage with the ladies. But aside from the fact that I work as a line cook and I live at home, I'm also an aspiring artist. A graphic artist. I mean, my dream job is to either work for a place like Marvel or DC illustrating their comic books and graphic novels, or to just create my own one day. But the moment you tell a girl that you like to draw comic books, they look at you like you just took a shit in front of them.

But I don't know Gemma, and since she's leaving tomorrow I don't have a lot to lose. Besides, something tells me she's different from the others, and it's not just her accent.

"I'm an artist," I tell her, deciding to cut out the aspiring crap. "Graphic design, graphic art. I sketch, I paint, lots of digital work. I'm in the middle of illustrating my own comic book, though I just have half the rough drawings complete and none of the dialogue. I've even applied for art school but I'm still waiting to hear back."

She's silent for a moment and I peer at her cautiously, expecting to see her eyes glazed over. Instead, she looks extraordinarily happy. Her smile is breathtakingly wide and it's such a sharp contrast to her ever-present smirk.

"Really?" she exclaims. "That's so awesome!"

"It is?" I thought she'd tolerate it, not actually think it was cool. Goddamn it, who just dropped this dream woman into my lap?

"I used to paint," she says and her smile winds down. A wash of sadness comes across her brow and I

279

have this sudden urge to kiss her and hope it brings that smile back.

I wait for her to elaborate, but she doesn't. "Hey," she says, brightening up. "Come on, I'll buy you another drink." She quickly downs her beer and I can tell she's forcing some cheer into her face. I can't say no to another bottle, though.

She grabs my hand again, but this time she's in no hurry to let go. Neither am I. Just like that, a beer is the last thing on my mind. This woman seems to be everything I'm looking for and I only have her for one night, if I even have her at all. I want to bring her into a dark corner and let my tongue caress hers before sliding it down her neck. I want to feel her smooth, tight body beneath my hands and make her smart mouth open with a moan. Then I want to glide my fingers down her pants and make her moan louder. I want her eyes to stare at me with lazy lust and beg me to do my worst.

But there are no dark corners on this roof deck, so we make our way through the sweaty mess of people again. I immediately miss the relative privacy and the invigorating chill of the outdoors and make up for it by having a cold beer, and then another.

We find a small living room at the end of the hall where we sit down on a couch and watch a few people play Rock Band in the near dark. I'm buzzed and the room is hypnotizing with the sounds and lights and her warmth beside me. I put my hand on her thigh and try to talk to her, but it's too loud and the dark is too inviting, too freeing. I go to whisper in her ear, to ask her if she's having a good time, to ask her what time her flight leaves, to ask her anything at all, and I find my lips grazing her earlobe. I'm losing the war and losing it fast.

She tastes far too good for me to stop. I tease the rim of her ear with my tongue to taste her even better.

She doesn't shove me away. She doesn't flinch. She just turns her head so my lips are next to hers, and for one moment I hesitate, my lips brushing lightly against hers, feeling the heady desire build to a breaking point. Her breath hitches in anticipation.

Then I kiss her. It's sweet and soft and so gentle that all the blood in my body doesn't know where to go.

Then it hurts.

"Ow," I say, pulling back slightly and rubbing my fingers over my mouth. What the hell?

"Sorry!" she whispers harshly, flushed from either embarrassment or arousal, and she quickly removes her fangs from her mouth, tossing them over her shoulder. "I forgot they were in there."

"Good thing we didn't start off with a blow job," I joke.

"No," she says deviously, and her hand goes on top of my erection. My eyes go wide. "That was going to come second."

"Was?" I repeat, feeling myself get harder under her touch. I can't even stand it.

She bites her lip coquettishly and once again I am wondering how the fuck I got so lucky. Must have been the eyeliner and dick comments.

I grab her face in my hands and kiss her, not gentle this time, not slow. It is fast and feverish and her mouth is even sweeter than the rest of her. She's a good kisser, but then again so am I, and I sink into this dizzy well of lust that I'm not sure how to get out of. So I don't even try.

We make out like that forever, my tongue exploring her mouth, fucking it hard and soft all at once, followed by my lips on her neck and her hand stroking my shaft. I think the last time I had a handjob over my clothes was in high school, but now there's something so fucking erotic about it that I have a hard time not coming.

Maybe it's the fact that there are five other people in the room, although they're all concentrating on playing "Helter Skelter." Still, voyeurism is a total turn-on.

I quickly remember that I had put a condom in my satchel because I figured that pretending to be a ripped, violent warrior might just be walking lady porn. I pull back, both of us breathing hard. "Want to find a room?" I say to her, my eyes glued to her wet, open mouth. Oh god, did I need those lips to finish me off.

She nods and gets up. I do the same, tucking myself up into the waist band of my briefs and making sure I'm not about to poke anyone's eye out. I take her hand and we leave the room and start exploring the hallway, though I have to press her up against the wall at least once and drive my tongue into her mouth and myself into her hip. I put my hand up her shirt and feel her soft skin through her thin, lacy bra, her nipples intoxicatingly hard. I want nothing more than to pinch them between my teeth and roll my tongue ring over them.

When I'm able to pry myself off of her again, we find a door that's locked. I'm not one to try and bust doors open, not even for the sake of hot monkey sex, so I take out my credit card and slide it up between the door and the frame. I breath out a sigh of relief as it clicks open and we stumble into a small billiards room that has been stuffed to the walls with furniture and breakables, all put away for the party.

I close the door behind us and lock it.

Made in the USA
Charleston, SC
19 November 2014